She Wasn't What He Expected.

Sure, she matched her physical statistics. All that information had been listed on her driver's license application, which had been included in the investigator's file on her. Still, something about her took him by surprise—something he couldn't quite put his finger on.

While he was studying her, Lisa was doing the same to him. The sun streaming in through the window behind him backlit his expensively cut hair—making him look like a golden boy. No, not a boy at all, she decided as she viewed the body so tastefully clothed in tailored slacks and a nautical-looking sweater. He had Wealth and Class stamped all over him, with capital letters.

"We were just leaving," Ellie reminded him.

"No, we weren't." He spoke to his grandmother while smiling at Lisa. "You were just about to tell me who this beautiful woman is."

Smooth, very smooth, Lisa thought. For some reason, his confidence irked her. "I'm Lisa Cantrell." She held out her ____ ___ ___ the grandson Ellie is always tal____ ____ ____ can charm the birds right ____

Bryce took her hand in hi____ ____ ____ are you, Lisa?"

"The kind that can't be charmed," she retort___

Dear Reader:

It takes two to tango, and we've declared 1989 the "Year of the Man" at Silhouette Desire. We're honoring that perfect partner, the magnificent male, the one without whom there would be no romance. From January to December, 1989 will be a twelve-month extravaganza, spotlighting one book each month as a tribute to the Silhouette Desire hero—our *Man-of-the-Month*!

You'll find these men created by your favorite authors utterly irresistible. March, traditionally the month that "comes in like a lion and goes out like a lamb," brings a hero to match in Jennifer Greene's Mr. March, and Naomi Horton's Slater McCall is indeed a *Dangerous Kind of Man*, coming in April.

Don't let these men get away!

Yours,

Isabel Swift
Senior Editor & Editorial Coordinator

CATHIE LINZ
As Good as Gold

Silhouette Desire
Published by Silhouette Books New York
America's Publisher of Contemporary Romance

SILHOUETTE BOOKS
300 East 42nd St., New York, N.Y. 10017

Copyright © 1989 by Cathie L. Baumgardner

ISBN: 0-373-05484-X

First Silhouette Books printing March 1989

Printed in the U.S.A.

Books by Cathie Linz

Silhouette Desire

Change of Heart #408
A Friend in Need #443
As Good as Gold #484

CATHIE LINZ

was in her mid-twenties when she left her career in a university law library to become a full-time writer of contemporary romantic fiction. In the six years since then, this Chicago author has had over a dozen romances published. An avid world traveler, she often uses humorous mishaps from her own trips as inspiration. In fact, the story for this book was a result of Cathie's recent trip to the Gold Rush country of California. After all the sight-seeing, she headed home to her two cats, her trusty word processor and her hidden cache of Oreo cookies!

Acknowledgments go to—

Grin and Bear It
Naperville, Illinois,
for their
retailing and teddy bear expertise

and

Jamestown Hotel,
Jamestown, California,
for answering my
many questions
and making
my stay there
so pleasant.

One

"If you have something to say—say it. If not, don't bother me, Colin." Bryce Stephenson directed the statement to his cousin without even looking up from the volume of *Illinois Revised Statutes* he was studying so intently. "I don't have the time for small talk today."

"You'd better make the time." Smiling his I-know-something-you-don't smile, Colin strolled into Bryce's law office. "Uncle Harold wants to see you in his office—pronto."

The news barely dented Bryce's concentration. "Tell him I'll stop by later," he said absently.

"Pronto means now, Bryce, as our uncle would tell you himself if you didn't keep disconnecting your phone." Bryce's continued preoccupation prompted Colin to add the clincher. "Hey, it's up to you. I just thought you might like to know that he's arranging to send you off to California...this afternoon, if not sooner."

"What?"

"Uncle Harold wants you in California by tonight."

"You're kidding?" But one look at Colin's face had him saying, "You're not kidding." With a sigh of resignation, Bryce marked his space and closed the statute book. This was one of the most annoying aspects of working in his illustrious family's law firm. Here at Stephenson, Stephenson, and Stephenson, family members were given unrestricted access into one another's offices. It wasn't a policy he approved of, but then he wasn't a policy-making senior partner. Not yet, anyway. Reminding himself that patience was a necessary virtue, Bryce removed his tortoiseshell reading glasses and tossed them onto the desk. "Okay, now what's this all about?"

"Family business."

"Isn't it always?" Bryce wearily rubbed the bridge of his nose. He'd been up half the night going over his notes for this case. "What's the problem this time?"

Colin shrugged. "I'll let Uncle Harold tell you the rest. He'll be angry as it is that I've stolen some of his thunder. Not that he was in a great mood to begin with." After perching on the corner of Bryce's oversize desk, Colin picked up an onyx paperweight and tossed it from one hand to the other. "I'm surprised you didn't hear the roar from in here."

Bryce took the paperweight away from him. "One of the advantages of having an office at the end of the hall."

"That, and the view."

Bryce glanced out at the Chicago skyline etched against the blue sky, and shrugged. "Who's got time to look at it?"

Colin nodded with mock sympathy. "Hey, being one of the best attorneys in Chicago is a tough job, but somebody's got to do it."

"Yeah, right." Bryce left his office, knowing that as soon as he was out of sight, Colin would probably take the opportunity to try out his swivel chair for size. Competitiveness was an inbred Stephenson trait, tempered only by family loyalty, which always came first. Colin wouldn't go out of his way to sabotage Bryce's position, but he would be eagerly waiting in the wings for Bryce to make a mistake.

As Colin had predicted, Harold Stephenson was not in the best of moods.

"You wanted to see me?" Bryce asked.

"I wanted to see you ten minutes ago. What took you so long? Your office may be in the hinterlands, but it can't take you that long to walk here! And why don't you ever answer your phone?"

Bryce didn't bother defending himself. Instead, he sat down in the leather chair facing the desk and got right to the point. "What's wrong?"

"It's that *woman* again!"

To Bryce's knowledge there was only one person who could provoke such agitation, such utter frustration in his usually unemotional uncle. "All right, what's Grandmother Ellie done now?"

"Her name is Eleanor, and she's not really your grandmother," Harold retorted, wiping at his brow with a monogrammed linen handkerchief.

"She's my grandfather's second wife and widow, which makes her my stepgrandmother, but you didn't call me in here to discuss the family tree, did you?"

"You'll have to go out there. There's nothing else to be done!" Harold pounded a fist on his ten-thousand-dollar antique desk. "I won't have it. Do you hear me? I won't have the family's good name—not to mention our money— thrown away by a foolish old woman! Eleanor has been nothing but trouble since the day my father met her. Marrying her was the biggest mistake he ever made, but then he was still in shock after my mother's death. Eleanor knew that and capitalized on it. She took advantage of him.''

Bryce didn't share his uncle's opinion of Ellie, but he knew it would be useless trying to reason with Harold while he was so upset. "Calm down. Your blood pressure must be going through the roof. Why don't you start at the beginning.''

"She's gotten hooked up with some con artist who's trying to fleece her, but of course Eleanor is too blind to see it. She's about to hand over hundreds of thousands of dollars to someone named—'' Harold paused to look down at the private investigator's report on his desk "—Lisa Cantrell, a woman who's gotten Eleanor all fired up with some pie-in-the-sky idea about opening a *toy* museum, of all things. But I've had this Lisa Cantrell checked out, and let me tell you, she's nothing more than a common con artist.'' Harold handed the thick file over to Bryce. "You'll have to go out there, find out exactly what's going on and put a stop to it. You're the only one Eleanor listens to, anyway. Agnes has you booked on a three o'clock flight out of O'Hare.''

"You'll have to have your trusty secretary cancel that plane reservation. I've got a court appearance this afternoon.''

"Ask for a continuance.''

"It's already been continued for almost a year.'' Seeing the flush rising in his uncle's face, Bryce said, "Don't worry, I'll go to California, but not until the end of the week. I'll need that much time to clear my schedule. This is, what, Monday? I'll leave Saturday morning.''

"Read what's in that folder and I think you'll leave sooner than that,'' Harold predicted.

Bryce left Thursday evening, but only after he'd won his case. Worn out by a week of too much work and not enough sleep, Bryce fell asleep in his business-class seat before the 747 had even taken off, and he didn't wake up until the plane landed in San Francisco.

As he removed his garment bag from the overhead bin, Bryce tried telling himself that a few days in the warm sun of California sounded nice after the chilly first week of April they'd just had in Chicago. But that reassurance disappeared once he realized it was just as chilly in San Francisco as it had been at home. Only here it was foggy as well. His vision was already blurry from exhaustion; he didn't need Mother Nature adding her two cents' worth.

Since he couldn't see more than a few feet in front of his rental car in this weather anyway, Bryce opted for spending the night in the nearest hotel. He'd resume his mission in the morning. For that's what this was; he had no misconceptions about that. He'd been sent on a mission to clean up this untidy family situation. He could almost hear his cousin Colin saying, "Hey, it's a tough job, but somebody's got to do it."

"That's not your job," Lisa Cantrell chided as she removed a feather duster from Ellie Stephenson's hand. "You're a customer here at The Toy Chest; you're not supposed to be working in the store."

"Nonsense." Ellie firmly took the feather duster right back. "You're busy checking that new order that just came in. A little bit of tidying isn't going to hurt me one bit. I may be a senior citizen, but I'm not decrepit yet, you know."

Lisa looked at Ellie and shook her head. Ellie's outfit—a trendy sweatshirt, blue jeans and running shoes—was hardly that of a matronly senior citizen. Lisa only hoped *she* looked as good when the time came for *her* to collect Social Security. "Don't try using that senior-citizen line on me. We both know you've got more energy than I do."

"Exactly." Ellie's smile brimmed with satisfaction.

"But that doesn't change the fact that you're a customer and shouldn't be working—"

"Now, don't nag, dear. Let a little old lady have some fun. You know I only do the dusting as an excuse to touch all these wonderful old toys. And if I don't dust them, they'll sit here all forlorn and forgotten while the new toys get all the attention."

Lisa threw out her hands in surrender. "All right, I give up. But if anyone comes in, tell them to wait a moment and I'll be right with them. I don't want you experimenting with the cash register again, Ellie. You remember what happened last time."

"We finally got the No Sale sign back down again, didn't we? How was I to know it would be temperamental? I had no trouble mastering the high tech register when I had that temporary job at McDonald's."

"There's more than a slight difference between punching in orders for Big Macs and handling a register that dates back to the 1890s," Lisa noted wryly. "Just call me if someone should come in, okay?"

"Okay, I will. Go on." Ellie shooed her away as if she were a pesky child. "You're the manager here—go manage those boxes."

It took Lisa awhile to unpack the order of teddy bear T-shirts, coffee mugs and cards. Although The Toy Chest sold all kinds of toys, she had recently added a corner devoted entirely to teddy bear paraphernalia. Sales were brisk, which pleased the store's absentee owner. As a result, Lisa had been given a raise and increasing amounts of authority over inventory and display, which pleased her. She took care of the store as if it were her own.

So did Ellie Stephenson, Lisa had to admit. The older woman came in at least once a week and fussed over the display case of antique toys. Lisa didn't consider it strange that Ellie spent so much time at the store. Their mutual interest in toys had progressed into a strong friendship. The truth was that Lisa welcomed Ellie's company. She'd even offered the woman a job as a part-time assistant, but to her surprise Ellie had gently turned it down. She'd told Lisa that what she *really* wanted to do was start a permanent display site for antique toys.

Lisa had loved the idea of a toy museum and did all she could to encourage Ellie to pursue her dreams. After all, dreaming was one area in which Lisa was an expert. She'd been doing it all her life, and twenty-six years of experience had to count for something.

Bryce was running behind schedule. He'd hoped to be in Jamestown by now; however, it looked as though his timetable would be off by at least an hour. That irritated him. He hated being wrong about anything.

At least he'd left the fog behind in San Francisco. It was clear and sunny here. But since he'd left the Interstate, his progress had been delayed by the highway's numerous curves, which made it difficult to exceed the thirty-five-mile-per-hour speed limit.

He passed apple groves in blossom on both sides of the road, but their beauty was lost on Bryce, who was speaking into a microcassette recorder. He figured there was no sense wasting time just driving along when he could be doing something productive like dictating notes for an upcoming speech before the Chicago Bar Association.

He arrived in Jamestown sixty-nine minutes behind schedule, but his good temper had been restored by the fact that he'd completed his speech. Now he directed all his attention to the next matter at hand—dealing with his free-spirited grandmother.

Since the city's Main Street extended only a few blocks, Bryce had no problem finding what he was looking for. The Toy Chest was in a building that could have come from the set of a TV western. Just as he'd expected, his grandmother was inside the store. He tapped on the plateglass window to get her attention. When Ellie looked up, he smiled and then entered the store.

"Bryce! What a surprise! What are you doing here?"

It took him a few seconds to realize that, between hugs, his grandmother was subtly trying to draw him back toward the door. Any doubts he might have had about coming were erased by Ellie's actions. Something was definitely going on here.

"I came to see you." He leaned down and dropped a kiss on a cheek that was both smooth and slightly wrinkled. But then that was Ellie, a study of opposites. "I had some business in the area, so I thought I'd drop in and pay you a visit. How are you?"

"Fine, fine. Surprised to see you. You say you drove here? All the way from Chicago?"

"No, I rented a car in San Francisco."

"Still, it's quite a long drive. You must be hungry. Let's go over to the café and you can tell me all about it over a piece of Rosie's homemade pie." She tugged on his arm again.

"There's no need to hurry." He paused to look at the display of mechanical toys she'd been dusting. "You go on with what you were doing. I can wait."

"Nonsense, I can do this anytime. It's not every day that I get an unexpected visit from my favorite grandson."

"I didn't realize you were actually working here."

"I'm not." Catching his pointed look at the feather duster in her hand, she hastily put it on the shelf, as if to distance herself from the cleaning tool. "I just help out occasionally. That's all."

"Why? You certainly don't need the money."

"There's more to life than just money," she reminded him sharply.

"Granted, but as we both know, money does come in handy now and again."

"You're getting cynical, Bryce."

"You noticed," he said with a pleased smile.

She shook her head in exasperation. "What am I going to do with you?"

"Talk to me."

"Fine. But not here."

Bryce was about to press Ellie further when he was interrupted by the sound of a woman's voice coming from the back of the store. "Do you need some help?" he heard her ask.

"No, thanks," he replied. "I think I can handle Ellie on my own."

"Bryce!" Ellie gave him a reprimanding look. "Don't worry, Lisa. He's not a customer. It's just my grandson who's come to see me." Ellie tugged on Bryce's arm. "Actually, we were just on our way out."

Bryce refused to budge. This young woman had to be the infamous Lisa Cantrell, and he wanted to get a better look at her. The private investigator had supplied him with photographs, but as Bryce saw Lisa for the first time, he had to admit that none of them had done her justice.

She wasn't what he expected. Sure, she matched her physical statistics—brown hair, blue eyes. Height, five foot seven. Weight, one hundred thirty pounds. All that information had been listed on her California driver's license application, which had been included in the investigator's file on her. Still, something about her took him by surprise—something he couldn't quite put his finger on.

While he was studying her, Lisa was doing the same to him. The sun streaming in through the window behind him prevented her from seeing his face, but it backlit his expensively cut blond hair—making him look like a golden boy. No, not a boy at all, she decided as she viewed the body so tastefully clothed in tailored slacks and a nautical-looking sweater. He had *Wealth* and *Class* stamped all over him, with capital letters.

"We were just leaving," Ellie reminded Bryce.

"No, we weren't." He spoke to his grandmother while smiling at Lisa. "You were just about to tell me who this beautiful woman is."

Smooth, very smooth, Lisa thought. For some reason, his confidence irked her. "I'm Lisa Cantrell." She held out her hand. Before he took it, she added, "So you're the grandson Ellie is always talking about, the one who can charm the birds right out of the trees."

Bryce took her hand in his. "And what kind of bird are you, Lisa?"

"The kind that can't be charmed," she retorted.

When he held on to her hand longer than was necessary, she narrowed her eyes and quickly but thoroughly looked him over. Now that the sun was no longer in her eyes, she could see him more clearly. His eyes were blue, and he was staring at her as intently as she was staring at him. He gave the impression that he was looking for something—something beneath the surface, something he didn't really approve of.

She could easily imagine that she'd done any number of things that a conservative Ivy Leaguer like him might not approve of. Telling herself she didn't care what he thought, she looked away.

Bryce was briefly disappointed that he could no longer see her eyes. They were the most unusual color, more gray than blue. The kind of eyes a man could get lost in if he wasn't careful. But Bryce hadn't reached the age of thirty-three without learning how to be very careful.

He felt her tug on her hand, belatedly reminding him that he was still hanging on to it.

"Sorry," he murmured, and with an apologetic smile released her hand.

Most women would have considered Bryce's smile irresistible, but it was a shade too practiced for Lisa's tastes. Glib-tongued charmers were not her type. They tended to say one thing while meaning another. She had the feeling that Bryce was doing that right now, and it made her uneasy. Why all this pretense? Why the strong disapproval she'd glimpsed in his eyes earlier?

"You're here in Jamestown to see your grandmother?" she asked.

"That's right." He put an arm affectionately around Ellie's shoulders.

"You shouldn't have come to the store today if you were expecting your grandson for a visit," Lisa told Ellie, fishing to see if Bryce's appearance had been anticipated.

"I wasn't expecting him," Ellie replied. "He took me by surprise."

Lisa was willing to bet that Bryce did that a lot—take people by surprise, after charming them first, of course.

"You're lucky he found you," she murmured, although she doubted luck had anything to do with it. Even though she'd only just met Bryce, she was already suspicious. Something about him didn't ring true. "By the way, how did you know to look for Ellie here?" she turned to ask him.

"Instinct," he replied with another confident smile.

Lisa's instincts told her that there was more to Bryce's visit than met the eye. She wondered what he was really up to.

She didn't have to wait long to find out. Later that afternoon, while Ellie was taking her customary siesta, Bryce returned on his own to The Toy Chest and confronted Lisa.

"So what's this nonsense about you and my grandmother opening a toy museum?"

Two

Bryce had chosen his words deliberately; they were meant to put Lisa on the defensive. He would have preferred to charm her into telling him the truth, but her earlier behavior indicated that she was wise to that tactic. She'd looked at him as if daring him to come out and say what he really meant. So he had. Now the ball was in her court.

She returned it with a stunning backhanded volley. "Ah, the charming attorney is finally getting to the point. What a refreshing change."

She was cool under pressure; he'd grant her that. "You didn't answer my question."

It escaped her why he should care if his grandmother had a dream of opening a toy museum. There was no law against that. "You'll have to be more specific in your examination, counselor. What in particular did you want to know about this *nonsense* concerning the toy museum?"

"Is it true?"

"Is what true?"

Everything listed in that inch-thick file I've got in my car, he was tempted to say, but restrained himself. He shouldn't lay too many of his cards on the table at once. "Are you and my grandmother involved in opening a toy museum?"

"Yes."

"Why?"

"Why not?"

"You seem determined to make this hard on me," he noted with a rueful smile that he knew always worked miracles on recalcitrant women.

It didn't appear to have any effect on Lisa, however. She just shrugged, returning his smile with one of her own.

Bryce decided to try another tack. "To tell you the truth," he admitted, "I'm concerned about my grandmother."

Now Lisa did become worried. Was there something wrong with Ellie? She seemed incredibly healthy, but appearances could be deceiving. "Is Ellie all right?"

"That's what I'm here to find out."

"She seems fine to me. In good spirits. She seems to have a lot of energy—"

"—and money," he interjected.

"She doesn't have any financial problems that I know of. Ellie does take on a temporary job every now and then, but they don't last very long. I think she does it more for the company than for the money. She doesn't get many visitors, you know." She gave him a chastising look. "It's a shame her family can't come out to visit her more often."

"So you'd have me believe that you aren't aware of the fact that my grandmother is a very wealthy woman?"

Very wealthy? Ellie? "I always figured she was doing all right, but—"

Bryce jumped in before she could complete her sentence. "She's doing more than just all right and you know it!"

"I do?"

He nodded. "Let's be frank."

"By all means."

"When we heard what my grandmother was planning to do with a such a large sum of money, the family naturally became concerned."

"Naturally." Lisa nodded with mock understanding.

"So how much is it going to cost?"

"The toy museum? I don't know exactly. We're still getting estimates."

"I'm not talking about the toy museum. I'm talking about you!" Frustration and anger were clearly apparent in both his voice and his glowering expression. "How much has my grandmother given you already, and how much is it going to cost to get rid of you?"

"More money than you'll ever earn," she retorted with a pleasant smile.

"So you admit that you're out to fleece my grandmother?"

"Naturally. I make a practice of fleecing grandmothers."

Bryce was at a loss. She didn't seem at all upset by his accusations. She seemed positively amused. "You're getting a kick out of this, aren't you?"

"Well, it's not every day that someone I've never met walks in and accuses me of trying to steal money from senior citizens, so I try to make the most of it when it does happen."

"There's nothing funny about this situation."

"If your accusations were true, you'd be right. It probably wouldn't be very funny. But since they aren't true, I can afford to laugh at them."

"I would think that if you were innocent, you'd be insulted and outraged at being accused of what I'm accusing you of."

"What good would that do?" she said with a good-natured practicality that was sure to drive him nuts. "You've obviously decided I'm guilty. My getting outraged about it would only fuel the fire."

"You're very clever. I'll grant you that."

"Why, thank you," she said dryly.

"But you don't fool me."

"Of course I don't. How rich is Ellie, anyway?

"Rich enough to own this store."

For the first time, Lisa did look shaken. "Ellie owns The Toy Chest?"

"Don't tell me you didn't know."

His disbelief jarred her back into resuming the mask of mocking humor. "I don't have anything else to tell you until I talk to Ellie. Our conversation is over for today. It's been fun, but I do have a store to manage."

"This isn't over," he told her.

"No, it certainly isn't. It won't be over until I get your apology in writing. I'll frame it and hang it over there, next to the very first dollar earned by The Toy Chest. *Then* this will be over."

"Don't bet on it." Bryce turned on his heel and stormed out of the store, almost running over a group of prospective customers in the process.

Later, as Lisa rang up the order of the tourists who'd come in to browse and ended up buying, she tried to ignore the questions churning through her mind. But once there was a lull in between customers, Lisa couldn't put it off any longer. Was Ellie really the owner of The Toy Chest? If so, why all the subterfuge? Why have Lisa send the store's progress reports to some address in Sacramento?

Sitting on a stool behind the counter, Lisa sipped tea from a teddy bear mug and tried to sort out her muddled thoughts. Those thoughts covered two topics—Ellie and Bryce.

She dealt with the subject of Bryce first. He'd seemed completely convinced of her guilt. Why? What had given him the idea that she was after Ellie's money, money she hadn't even known Ellie possessed? It didn't make sense. Unless he was just being paranoid. Lisa's own run-ins with the rich and powerful had taught her that they were extremely protective of their wealth. After all, she'd married into a wealthy family at the young age of eighteen and learned to her own misfortune that their money was more important to them than anything else.

There was no avoiding the fact that Bryce Stephenson's little visit had given her a feeling of déjà vu, bringing up memories she'd rather forget. Another time, another place, when another man had offered to buy her off...after she and his son had eloped. Then she'd been all the things Bryce had mentioned—outraged, angered, insulted. And hurt. Incredibly hurt. But she didn't want to dwell on that now.

Instead, she deliberately focused her thoughts on Ellie. Lisa had always considered herself to be a good judge of character; she'd been burned in the past enough not to repeat her mistakes. Trust no longer came easily to her, but once she believed in someone...the way she believed in Ellie...

Lisa rubbed her temples in an attempt to stave off the headache that was taking root there. It didn't make any sense. Why would Ellie have lied about owning the store? Not that she had ever actually said she *didn't* own the store; the question had just never arisen. Or had Bryce been the one who'd lied? But why should he? And what about his claim that Ellie was rich? She certainly didn't act like someone with a lot of money. Someone wasn't telling the truth here—was it Bryce or Ellie?

The sound of the bell tinkling as the store's front door opened had Lisa putting on a welcoming smile. It was El-lie.

Since it was almost closing time anyway, the older woman flipped the Open sign over to its Closed side. "We need to talk, Lisa."

"First tell me if what Bryce said is true. Are you really the owner of The Toy Chest?"

Ellie's guilty expression was answer enough. "I never wanted you to find out this way. Bryce had no right to tell you."

It wasn't until that moment that Lisa realized part of her had still been holding out hope that this had all been a mis-take; that Ellie was just what she appeared to be—a straightforward woman who was as honest as the day was long. So much for that daydream, Lisa thought ruefully.

"I wanted to tell you myself," Ellie was saying.

Lisa felt betrayed. "Then why didn't you? Why keep it a secret? Why come in the store all the time and act like you're nothing more than an interested customer, when you're really the owner? Why have me send all the accounting and sales information to an address in Sacramento?" Her voice, which had been raised in anger, now became husky with disappointment. "I don't understand."

"Let me try to explain." Ellie touched Lisa's hand in a gesture of regret and remorse. "It seemed so harmless at the time. I liked the idea of opening a toy store, but I didn't want to handle the details involved with running it. So I hired a firm in Sacramento to find me a manager to run the store. I'd closed up the house here in Jamestown and was living down in Palm Springs at the time. When I saw from the reports how well you were managing the store, I became curious to see it for myself. I should have told you then, but I didn't want you to think I was checking up on you, that I didn't trust you to manage the store. In the beginning all I was going to do was stop by, but when I returned to Jamestown I realized how much I'd missed living here. So I moved back."

"Why didn't you tell me then, that first time that you came to the store, that you were the owner?"

"Because, frankly, I don't like the responsibility of being the one in charge. I thought you would ask me questions I didn't have the answers to. I'd never run a store before—what did I know? And later, once we got to know each other, well...I enjoyed the relationship we had. I thought that relationship wouldn't be the same if you knew I was the owner and not just a strange lady who came in to dust the old toys once a week."

"I never thought you were strange," Lisa said in denial.

"Are you very angry with me?" Ellie asked somewhat hesitantly.

"I'm hurt that you didn't trust me with the truth."

"I intended to tell you. In fact, you should be getting a letter from the office in Sacramento saying that the owner wants to arrange a meeting with you. You see, I didn't want any misunderstandings between us when I told you that I'd like you to head the toy museum."

Lisa looked at her in surprise. "Me?"

"You."

The certainty in Ellie's eyes made Lisa say, "This toy museum isn't just a dream for you, is it."

"It's a dream I can afford."

The light was dawning. "You *are* rich, aren't you?"

"Afraid so."

"Very rich?"

Ellie nodded. "Actually, the money belonged to my dear departed husband, Samuel Stephenson. I was his second wife. His children never approved of our marriage, never approved of me. The Stephenson family is very elitist. Old money, a family tree that goes back to the arrival of the *Mayflower*. I was Samuel's private nurse, and fourteen years younger than he. I didn't measure up, in their eyes. They thought I was some kind of gold digger who'd married him for his money. After Samuel's death, things became pretty chilly. To this day they still haven't really accepted me. Bryce is the one who's been the closest to me—which is why they sent him out, I'm sure.

"Who sent him?" Lisa asked.

"The head of the family, Samuel's oldest son, Harold."

"Bryce's father?"

"Heavens no. His uncle. Bryce's parents were killed when he was quite young. Harold and his wife took Bryce in and raised him along with their own son, Edward. Edward is several years older than Bryce, but Bryce has always been the one they send to deal with me. He's a dear boy, but I don't want him interfering with my plans for this toy museum."

Beneath the annoyance Lisa could hear the affection in Ellie's voice. "He's your favorite, isn't he?"

"Yes," Ellie admitted. "Edward takes after his father and rarely even speaks to me. My other grandson, Colin, was just a teenager the last time I saw him. His father is Harold's younger brother, and Harold keeps them all firmly under his thumb."

"Including Bryce," Lisa pointed out.

Ellie came to his defense. "Bryce feels he owes his uncle because Harold took him in when his parents died. He works in the family's law firm, but he's made his own place in the legal world. I'm actually quite proud of him—when

I'm not furious with him, that is. I know what kind of sticky spider webs the Stephenson family weaves, but they have no right to draw you into it. This is family business.''

"There's something else that's been bothering me. What would make your family think I was trying to con you into giving me money? Because I work in the store?''

"No, because I've recently moved some of my funds around in preparation for starting the toy museum. I put your name as the cosigner on that account.''

"Ellie, you shouldn't have done that without talking to me first!''

Ellie held out her hands in a placating gesture. "I only did it a few days ago. I still have the bank forms for you to sign in my purse. I was going to talk to you about it all when I discussed the toy museum and my being the owner of the store here.'' She frowned. "Unfortunately Harold beat me to it. Not that there's anything he can do to stop me, but that won't prevent him from trying. I've always suspected that he's hired a private detective to keep tabs on me.''

"Do you think Harold would have had me investigated, too?''

"Probably, but you've got nothing to be afraid or ashamed of.''

Lisa ruefully shook her head. "You may feel that way, but I doubt the Stephensons would agree with you. I'll bet that's why your grandson came in here so fired up about buying me off. As you know, I haven't exactly led a conventional life. Neither have my parents, for that matter.''

"Neither have I,'' Ellie added. "That's why I like you so much.''

Lisa had to smile. She could empathize with what Ellie had been through with the Stephensons. She knew what it was like to be labeled a "gold digger.'' It reassured her to think she hadn't been such a bad judge of character after all—she and Ellie did have a lot in common.

"I have to say that you seem to be taking this very calmly," Lisa noted.

"So are you, dear," Ellie said admiringly. "Bryce actually accused you of trying to get money from me?" She shook her head in amazement. "What a foolish boy. Did you set him straight?"

"I laughed in his face," Lisa retorted, "which didn't please him one bit. He said if I was really innocent I would have been outraged and not been amused."

"How like a Stephenson to decide how someone else should react in a situation. Individuality is definitely frowned upon."

"So what happens now?"

"Nothing. Bryce will return to Chicago in a few days, having felt that he's done his duty by his uncle but unable to convince me to change my mind."

"You sound pretty sure of that. Has this happened before?"

Ellie shook her head. "Usually Bryce just phones and tries to talk me out of doing something. This is the first time he's actually come all the way out here."

"Probably became desperate when he saw my file," Lisa muttered.

She could easily imagine what fiascos it would contain. Her short-lived marriage and the subsequent divorce. She was sure that if they talked to her former in-laws, the term "gold digger" was included in the report. Then there had been that little incident at the pet store she'd worked in when she was twenty. That would make fascinating reading as well. And how about her parents' current project? Gold prospecting was not exactly a steady profession. There was no getting around it; some of the black-and-white facts of her life could be used to paint a very misleading picture. And while there was little that Lisa hadn't already told Ellie during the course of their friendship, she didn't think the superior-sounding Stephensons would be as understanding.

She knew it was useless getting angry about it now. There was no way to repair the damage that had been done, no way to restore the privacy that had been invaded. But the anger didn't go away; it just went underground, waiting for something to set it off.

Bryce's next visit did exactly that. He was waiting outside the store for her the next morning before she'd even opened up.

"So—" Lisa reached into her tote bag for the keys to the store "—you've come to offer me my apology. And so early in the day. How sweet of you."

"Apology nothing. I'm here to try and talk some sense into you. I can forgive Ellie having her head in the clouds. She's sixty-eight. But there's no excuse for your cavalier behavior."

She whirled to face him, "Listen, buster, you can insult me all you want, but I don't want to hear one word against Ellie!" Lisa jabbed her finger at Bryce's chest, emphasizing her point. "She's a wonderful lady. Too damn good to be your grandmother, if you ask me. She may have her head in the clouds, but she's got her feet planted firmly on the ground and I resent your insinuation that just because she's sixty-eight she's incapable of making her own decisions about her own life."

Bemused by her response, Bryce had nothing to say at first. This was the firebrand reaction he'd been expecting when he'd first confronted her yesterday. He knew she was a woman of passion. It was there in her wonderful eyes— fire, fury, intensity.

It also didn't escape his notice that she hadn't gotten angry on her own behalf, only on Ellie's. Whatever else Lisa Cantrell was, she was certainly loyal to Ellie.

"So I don't want to hear another word about Ellie being incapable. You got that?"

He nodded, a secret smile of appreciation lifting his lips. "I've got that."

"Good. Now, come inside. There's something I want to discuss with you."

The smile left his face. Just when he started doubting her guilt, she said something to get it going again. "Are you ready to come to terms?"

She set her purse behind the counter before answering. "I want the report that your uncle's private investigator did on me."

Her words left Bryce wondering if he'd ever regain his equilibrium. "I don't know what you're talking about."

"Come on. I'm not stupid. Neither is Ellie. We both know that your uncle is having her movements watched. If it was up to me I'd sue the pants off you for invasion of privacy. But Ellie feels she can handle Harold's obsessive behavior. That's her decision. Mine is that I don't want to provide leisure reading for a batch of paranoid weirdos. So hand over the report. And consider yourself lucky that I'm not suing you on my own behalf."

"You're certainly a tough lady, aren't you? I wonder what made you that way."

"Don't try to figure me out," she said quietly. "There's more to me than can be explained in some neat little report."

"I'm getting that impression." His voice was equally quiet.

"So, are you going to give me the report or not?"

"Not. But I can assure you that if such a report does exist—and I'm not saying it does—it's *not* being used as leisure reading material for a bunch of paranoid weirdos." Laughter was apparent in his voice.

"Then what is it being used for?"

"I couldn't say."

"Couldn't? You *won't* say. There's a difference." She sighed. "You're going to be difficult about this, aren't you?"

"I could say the same about you."

"And you have," she pointed out.

"Maybe it would help if you told me your side of the story."

"*Story* being the operative word here. You've already made up your mind about me."

"I thought I had," he readily admitted, "but I have to confess that you've got me stymied, and that's not something that happens to me very often. So, come on. Tell me about this toy museum."

Lisa reluctantly did so. "Despite what you think, I had no idea that Ellie was wealthy, let alone that she owned The Toy Chest. When she talked about the toy museum, I didn't realize that it was a dream she was capable of fulfilling on her own. I'm not used to dreams being satisfied that easily.

"Anyway, I supported her, encouraged her in the idea of the museum. I thought it was a good idea. I still do. We talked about pooling our own collections as a basis for the museum's collection, about acquiring additional items."

"My grandmother told me that she wants to put you in charge of the entire museum project," he remarked.

"She told me the same thing yesterday."

"What qualifications do you have to be heading such a project?"

"Aside from the ability to run a scam on rich older women, you mean?"

Having grown accustomed to Lisa's somewhat acerbic sense of humor, he smiled at her and said, "Yes. Aside from that."

"I'm sure it's all in your little report."

"I want to hear it from you."

But Lisa was leery of complying with his request. She'd learned the hard way that no number of heated protests of innocence could sway someone who'd already convicted you in his own mind. Trying to convince Bryce that she was innocent would mean admitting that his opinion mattered to her—and she wasn't ready to do that. Keeping her distance kept her safe. Not caring prevented her from caring too much. It was a system she'd developed over the years and it worked for her. She wasn't about to give it up now.

"Your grandmother is satisfied with my qualifications, and that's all that matters," she maintained.

"Is it?" His voice held a new intensity that was reflected in his eyes. He was looking at her, really looking at her, in a way that had nothing to do with suspicions and everything to do with attraction. "Is that really all that matters?"

"Yes, it is." She tore her gaze away with great difficulty. Had she not known better, she might have been tempted to believe he really was interested in her. But she did know better. The looks, the soft inflection, they were all tricks to con her into trusting him.

Determined to show him she wasn't fooled, she said, "So what do you plan on reporting back to your Uncle Harold?"

"I haven't decided what to tell my family, because I haven't decided what to make of you. But I plan on staying until I do figure you out. I never have been able to resist puzzles." Bryce had to admit that he was also finding it hard to resist this woman with her tigerish eyes and mocking sense of humor. Lisa Cantrell intrigued him. He'd never met anyone like her.

No, Bryce thought, he wouldn't be leaving just yet. Not until he'd figured out exactly what was going on—with her, and with him.

Three

***

Bryce spent all day Sunday with his grandmother, trying to pump her for information. He got nowhere. So he decided on a more direct approach.

"Tell me more about this friend of yours," he requested as he and Ellie sat down to breakfast on Monday morning.

"Which friend?" Ellie asked with deliberate blankness.

"Lisa Cantrell."

"Would you like Cornflakes or oatmeal?"

Grimacing at the hot cereal, a favorite of Ellie's but not of his, he reached for the cereal box. "I'll have Cornflakes. But to get back to my question—"

"It won't work, you know," Ellie stated as she calmly poured milk over her oatmeal.

"What won't?"

"You're not going to talk me out of opening this toy museum, so why don't you just sit back and enjoy yourself until you have to return to your hectic law office in Chicago. When *are* you going back to Chicago, by the way?''

"Trying to get rid of me already?" Bryce inquired dryly. "I only arrived two days ago."

"Nonsense." She fondly patted his hand. "You know I'm not trying to get rid of you. I always enjoy seeing you. But I know how busy you are. I realize you don't have time to spare and that you can't stay long."

Bryce decided this was as good a time as any to make his announcement. He'd already called the office and made arrangements. "Actually, I've got two weeks' vacation coming, and I've decided to spend it here."

"Really, Bryce, there's no need for you to waste your vacation checking up on me—or on Lisa for that matter. I can assure you that I know what I'm doing. I don't know what Harold has told you, but surely you realize how paranoid the man is."

Ellie's statement brought to Bryce's mind his phone conversation with Harold earlier that morning.

"What have you found out?" his uncle had asked him.

"Not much. So far, Ellie insists on going ahead with her plans for the toy museum."

"And this Cantrell woman? What do you make of her?"

"I don't know yet, but I plan on finding out."

"Good, good. I knew sending you out there was the right thing to do. The family has always had to be on the lookout for this kind of thing, people trying to take advantage of our goodwill and our money. One really can't be too careful. Remember that, Bryce."

The sound of Ellie's voice brought Bryce's attention back to the present.

"I know Harold is your uncle," she was saying, "but don't let that blind you to his faults—and he's got plenty! For one thing, he makes Scrooge look like a philanthropist. However, that's his problem, not mine. And despite what Harold may think or say, I am not senile, I am not stupid and I am not gullible.''

"I never said you were."

"But you've thought it."

Bryce shook his head. "The only thing you are is soft-hearted, which is why I worry about you."

"Don't. There's no need to worry about me."

"If there's nothing to worry about," he pointed out, "then there's no reason for you to mind that I'm sticking around for the next two weeks."

Ellie shook her head at his engaging smile. "You always were a charmer. Stubborn, too. Just like your grandfather."

"You still miss him, don't you."

Ellie's hazel eyes misted over as she nodded. "It's been five years now, but it seems like just yesterday that we were together. That's one of the reasons why I came back to Jamestown, you know. We spent some of our happiest times in the house here."

"I know. This is a large house for just one person, though."

"Is that why you were so upset when I reopened the house and moved back from Palm Springs?"

"I thought that you were happy in the condo there."

"I prefer it here. You're not the only one who can be stubborn, you know."

Bryce smiled. "I'm beginning to realize that."

"Then you should also realize that you won't be able to convince me to live the life of a proper Palm Springs matron. Look, if you'd like, I'll send Harold a note saying you did everything in your power to convince me to change my mind but it just didn't work. That should get you off the hook."

"What makes you think I'm so subservient to my uncle?" Bryce couldn't help sounding irritated. "Has it occurred to you that I might be concerned about you, and that's why I came to visit you? You're planning on entrusting a great deal of money to a virtual stranger. What do you really know about Lisa Cantrell? It's come to my attention that one of her former employers accused her of stealing. Were you aware of that?"

"Certainly. You're referring to that little incident at the pet store in…St. Louis, I think it was. Yes, I know all about that."

Bryce looked at his grandmother in disbelief. "Yet you still trust her?"

"*I* know what happened, but I doubt you do. The pet store where she was assistant manager wasn't taking proper care of the animals they were selling. Lisa reported the store to the humane society, which took action against the owners. That's when Lisa was accused of stealing and fired. The real reason she lost her job was because she blew the whistle on the unfit owners. The accusation of stealing was pure fabrication. The owners never pressed charges against her; they just blacklisted her in the city's retailing community."

"That's what she told you, but how can you be sure she's telling the truth?"

"Because I know Lisa. You really must learn to judge people by who they are, Bryce, and not be what the statistics say. After all, look at the statistics about me. Fourteen years younger than your grandfather, his nurse. On paper it looks quite suspicious. But I loved Samuel very much, just as he loved me. Something like that doesn't fit onto a neat little tabulation sheet. Harold never understood it, and he never will. I like to think there's still hope for you, though, Bryce. You made up your own mind about me. Do the same about Lisa."

"I still say it's natural that your family is concerned about protecting your best interests under these circumstances."

"It is my money," she reminded him gently. "The mistakes are mine to make."

"Money doesn't last long if you don't take care of it."

Ellie gave a long-suffering sigh. "This isn't going to be another lecture on financial responsibility, is it? It's not necessary, I can assure you. I still have nightmares from the last lecture you gave me. Decaying dollar bills were chasing me wherever I went. It wasn't a pretty sight, I can tell you."

"At least delay your plans for the museum until I can check Lisa out."

"It sounds like your uncle has already checked Lisa out, but I don't want to hear about it."

"At least tell me why you trust her so much."

Ellie shook her head. "It should be enough that I *do* trust her."

It wasn't enough for Bryce, but he could see he wasn't going to change Ellie's mind. What's more, his grandmother obviously had no intention of giving him any clues about the puzzle that was Lisa Cantrell. He'd have to put the pieces together himself.

Lisa was running late. She would have liked to blame Bryce for stubbornly remaining in her thoughts and distracting her from the matters at hand, but the truth was that she always seemed to be racing against the clock. Time was forever getting away from her. She should have left The Toy Chest ten minutes ago. Stuffing a pile of notes into her oversize bag, she grabbed her sunglasses from the counter and rushed out the store's front door, where she promptly ran into Bryce.

The near collision left her breathless. His hands on her arms prevented her from falling, but when she looked into his eyes . . . For some reason she felt herself slipping. He's trouble, she hastily reminded herself. Nothing but trouble.

Her equilibrium restored, she pretended not to notice the way his fingers lingered, warming her skin. Stepping away, she broke their physical contact before it could distract her any further.

His gaze remained where his hands couldn't. "Where are you off to in such a hurry?"

Lisa had no trouble reading his expression. He really did have this attraction thing down pat. She faced him without blinking, her stare a direct challenge. She'd expected him to look away, become flustered—something. Instead, his eyes crinkled at the corners as amusement entered their depths. That's when *she* became flustered. She ended their visual tug of war by putting on her sunglasses.

"I'm late for an appointment," she said.

"What appointment?"

"I've got to meet an antique toy dealer in Amador City by eleven-thirty."

"Who's going to mind the store while you're gone?"

"My assistant, Judy. Why?"

He shrugged, drawing her attention to his broad shoulders. "No reason. It was just a simple question."

"None of your questions are simple," she retorted. "They all have hidden meaning and suspicion behind them."

"Now you sound paranoid. What are you afraid of?"

"Heights and snakes," she answered obligingly. "Sneaky questions from attorneys are just annoying, not frightening." She was disconcerted by his laughter. "Look, much as I'd love to stand here and continue this pointless discussion, I do have an appointment to keep." She moved away.

He followed. "I'll come with you."

That stopped her. "Why?"

"Because I'm interested."

Interested. He'd said the word with just enough innuendo that he could have meant he was interested in her, but then again he might not have meant that at all. Just in case he had meant it, she gave him a deliberately discouraging look. "You don't want to come with me."

"I don't? Why not?"

"Well, for one thing...I'm driving."

"So? What's wrong with that?"

"Nothing. But I drive a VW bug that doesn't have much room." She shook her head at the idea of him fitting his six-foot-plus frame into her car. "I don't think you'd be very comfortable."

"Then we can go in my rental car. It's got a lot of room."

"I prefer to drive myself," Lisa said.

"Like being in the driver's seat, do you? I can understand that. No problem. I'll just follow you in my car."

"If you insist, but I think you'll find it a very boring experience."

"I doubt that," he murmured to himself as she took off toward her car. Boring was not a word that applied to Lisa Cantrell or anything she did. Unpredictable, fiery, unconventional—yes. And sexy as hell, he noted as a sudden gust of wind blew her full skirt up around her legs à la Marilyn Monroe. No experience with Lisa would be boring, not when she had legs like that! With a grin Bryce got into his car and followed her before she got away.

As Lisa drove north to Amador City, she was very much aware of the dark Buick in her rearview mirror. Or, more specifically, she was very much aware of the man in that car. She glanced at his reflection once again. Bryce looked the same as he had a moment ago. He was wearing mirrored sunglasses that made him look very... Very what? she asked herself. Very sexy, very upper crusty, very *California*?

"All of the above," she murmured aloud while punching in another station on her car radio.

She wasn't in the mood to hear a love ballad. She turned up the volume on something loud and distracting.

She was not going to allow herself to become distracted by Bryce Stephenson. He wasn't even really her type. Since her disastrous marriage she'd avoided rich men like the plague. And she preferred men with dark hair. She looked in her rearview mirror again. Actually, Bryce's hair was dark blond, she noted thoughtfully... maybe light brown.

Shaking her head, she resolutely looked forward again. Her future was ahead of her, not behind her. She should be concentrating on how to convince the antique toy dealer that Ellie's toy museum would be an ideal place to donate some of his pieces.

Still... Her eyes darted to the rearview mirror one more time. Why was she so preoccupied with Bryce Stephenson? Because he'd accused her of trying to fleece Ellie? It hadn't been the most auspicious of beginnings. And certainly not the way to make a good impression on her. He'd obviously switched tactics. Now he was going out of way to be nice to her, which meant he was up to something. He'd told her as much himself the other morning, when he'd said he planned on staying... until he'd figured her out.

"Smarter men have tried and failed," she murmured with a jaunty grin at his reflection in the mirror. "So go ahead and try to charm me. It won't work."

"Not much of a town, is it?" Bryce remarked as he joined Lisa on the sidewalk in Amador City.

She supposed she shouldn't have been surprised that he didn't notice the town's quaint beauty. But that didn't stop her from trying to open his eyes to his surroundings. "Amador City is the smallest incorporated city in California. And very proud of that fact. Last I heard, the population was 202 people. The buildings lining the main street here date back to the late 1800s.''

"Like the buildings in Jamestown."

So he had paid attention to the dates proudly displayed on the various buildings back in Jamestown. "That's right. Feel free to look around while I conduct my business. I don't think the subject of toys is one you'd care much about."

"On the contrary. The subject fascinates me."

There he went again, saying it as though *she* fascinated him.

"I doubt that toys are what you're really interested in," she retorted.

"Why do you say that? After all, I was a kid once..."

"Really?"

"...and I've played with my share of toys."

"Probably more than your share, but that's not important." She relented slightly. "All right, you can come inside and I'll introduce you, but then you'll have to leave. I don't want you interfering with the negotiations."

"What negotiations?"

"The owner of this store has quite a collection of his own. There's a chance he might be interested in participating in the toy museum once we get it going. And he has an antique rocking horse that we're very interested in obtaining."

"What for? The Toy Chest only sells new toys."

"We'd be obtaining it for the museum, not the store."

She sounded sincere, Bryce thought as he stood back and watched while Lisa and the toy store owner waxed enthusiastic over the subject of toys. She sounded as if she knew what she was talking about, but then he was no expert. So he waited to see how the dealer, who apparently *was* an expert, treated Lisa. The man spoke to her—and, more important, listened to her—as an equal. So her knowledge of toys was no con.

Actually Bryce hadn't been able to discover anything counterfeit about Lisa so far. She'd certainly been direct in her dealings with him, looking him straight in the eye when speaking to him, never floundering for an answer. Yet he knew that these traits were also the signs of a good con artist.

Catching sight of his preoccupied look, Lisa interrupted her conversation with the toy dealer to speak to Bryce. "Why don't you go ahead and look around town. We should be done here in half an hour."

But Bryce didn't want to leave. He wanted to learn more about her, and he couldn't do that strolling around town.

"Do you mind if I stay?" Bryce directed his question to the toy dealer.

The dealer shook his head. "I don't mind. Hate to let her out of your sight, eh?"

"Something like that," Bryce agreed.

Lisa tried to restrain her anger. It was clear to her that Bryce didn't trust her. What did he think she was going to do? Rob the cash register? Shoplift? And how was she supposed to negotiate intelligently while Bryce was breathing down her neck? He made her feel self-conscious, he made her furious, and he made her think about him when she should be thinking about business.

It was all she could do not to heave a sigh of relief when Bryce ambled toward the back of the store, giving her some much-needed breathing space. She was feeling slightly more generous toward him after the deal with the toy store owner had been successfully completed with promises for future donations to the museum.

"All done," she announced as she joined Bryce in the back of the store, where he was studying a display of toy soldiers.

"Good. I'm starving. How about lunch?"

"All right. There's a little place around the corner that serves great food."

When they arrived at the restaurant, Bryce glanced around with a wry look. Only then did he realize that she hadn't been kidding when she'd referred to it as a little place. Longer than it was wide, it was a small mom-and-pop operation.

Lisa noticed Bryce's look. "What's the matter, counselor? Too commonplace for you?"

"Not at all."

"Good. Because this place has some of the best food in the county."

After their order had been taken, Lisa looked over Bryce's left shoulder and absently noted, "It's sort of strange seeing ice-cream sundaes being served at the same bar where prospectors drank their whisky and laid their gold dust down. I guess that's progress for you."

Bryce looked confused. "What are you talking about?"

"That counter over there. It dates back to the gold rush days."

Bryce hadn't paid much attention, but now that she'd pointed it out, he realized that the counter was actually an intricately carved saloon bar.

"You've got a real eye for detail," he noted.

"I've got a soft spot for that period of history," she readily admitted. "It was an age of adventure, a time when the possibilities were endless and the proverbial pot of gold was promised at the end of every rainbow. Almost a hundred thousand people came west in just two years. It was the greatest gold rush of all time."

"It's hard to believe that claims of gold could make people act so impulsively, isn't it? A good example of herd mentality."

Lisa shook her head. "I can see you're obviously not the gold-at-the-end-of-the-rainbow type."

"What type am I, then?"

"The type who uses charm as a tool to get what he really wants, the type who's used to having things his own way."

"And you've discovered all that about me in just one afternoon? Very impressive," he said. "Incorrect, of course, but impressive."

"You don't think you're charming? Or you don't think you're used to having things your own way?"

"I can't answer that question, on the grounds that I might incriminate myself."

"That's a lawyer for you. Always evading the issue."

"What issue? I thought we were just sitting here, enjoying our lunch and sharing some polite conversation. But if you want to talk issues, fine. The environment, deficit spending, foreign affairs—take your pick."

Lisa couldn't help smiling. "What's this? A sense of humor? In an attorney? I thought that was illegal."

"It is."

She laughed.

"So the gold rush is one of your soft spots, hmm? Tell me more," he invited her.

"About the gold rush? Sure. It began in 1848, when gold was discovered in—"

"I meant tell me more about your other soft spots."

"That's privileged information, counselor."

"Meaning I'll have to find out for myself." Bryce smiled as if relishing the prospect. "Fair enough. So tell me, how long have you had this obsessive interest in the gold rush?"

"Blame it on my parents. They've always been fascinated by that period of history. And as I'm sure you already know from that little report of yours, they're currently involved with a gold-prospecting operation." Would he show surprise at her parents' activities, the way most outsiders did when hearing about it for the first time?

"Really?" He didn't look surprised, but he did look interested. "That's unusual."

"I come from an unusual family." She paused to nibble on a french fry. "You know, it occurs to me that you know everything there is to know about me, while all I know about you is that you're a successful attorney from Chicago who likes his cheeseburgers done medium rare."

"Ask away," he invited her. "My life's an open book."

"Yeah, right."

"I mean it."

"Come on. Don't make me play Twenty Questions. Tell me about yourself."

"Okay, here are the high points. I was born thirty-three years ago, on June twentieth, to be exact. I grew up, attended prep school, graduated, attended Northwestern University, graduated, attended Northwestern Law School, graduated, and joined my family's law firm nine years ago."

"That's it? That's your life?"

"In a nutshell, yes."

"How about without the nutshell?"

"Let's see.... I was an only child. My parents died when I was eight. My father's older brother, Harold, took over my care and sent me to boarding school with his son, Edward."

"Right away? You were sent to boarding school when you were only eight years old?"

He nodded, surprised by the disapproval in her voice.

"That's inhumane!"

"I enjoyed it," he said somewhat defensively. "It made me very self-reliant."

"Self-reliant? When you work in your *family's* law firm?"

"Tradition is a strong bond in our family. My grandfather started the firm, then his three sons took over, and now all three of their sons are in the firm. We're third-generation lawyers."

"So you're saying you always wanted to be a lawyer? Never a circus clown or a firefighter or a scientist?"

"I always knew the law was for me. Practicing for nine years has only confirmed that conviction."

"What kind of law do you practice?"

He grinned. "Good law."

"Very funny."

"The firm itself has attorneys who handle every type of law. I head the corporate division, but it seems that most of my time lately has been spent on a major construction project in the city and dealing with the various developers involved."

"You're not planning any development schemes out here, are you?" she asked suspiciously.

"No, I've got plenty in Chicago to keep me busy."

"I'm sure you do." She smiled sweetly. "Are you returning there soon?"

"You mean Ellie didn't tell you?"

"Tell me what?"

"I've taken two weeks vacation, and I've decided to stick around here for a while."

"What for?"

"That's what my grandmother asked me. I can't help wondering why you're both so eager to get rid of me."

"And we can't help wondering why you're so eager to stay," she retorted. "There are plenty of better places to spend your vacation. How about Hawaii? Or, better yet, Fiji?''

"I've already been to Hawaii. And Fiji."

"Ah, a world traveler. Then you'll get bored here very quickly. This region may be picturesque, but it lacks the kind of fast-paced excitement I'm sure you're used to. We actually lead very quiet lives around here. Are you going to eat that pickle?"

He shook his head.

"Then can I have it?"

"You may lead a quiet life, but I'm sure I won't be bored." He leaned closer and offered her a bite of his pickle. "Not with you around to keep me on my toes."

"Is that what I do?" She dabbed at her chin with a napkin. "Keep you on your toes?"

He nodded, his gaze remaining fixed on her parted lips. "It's one of the things you do." His eyes met hers. "I'm looking forward to discovering the rest of the things you do."

He was doing it again, she thought. Giving her one of *those* looks. It was becoming harder and harder for her to look away, but she did. "What about you?"

"What about me?"

"What do you do when you're not being a lawyer or your grandmother's keeper?"

He smiled. "Those two jobs keep me pretty busy."

"Oh, a workaholic."

"Maybe you can cure me," he quipped.

"I doubt that."

"You never know until you try."

There was a brief moment when Bryce thought he'd gotten through to her. One moment, suspended in time, when their eyes met and something...some sort of spark...flared between them.

But just when he thought he was getting somewhere, she said, "Are you going to eat the rest of your fries?"

He sat back with a sigh, wondering whether she'd been eyeing him—or his lunch. "Do you usually eat this much?"

"I don't usually eat lunch, so I'm making the most of it."

"You're not going to have room to eat that walnut pie you ordered."

"The pies here are homemade. I'll have room," she assured him with a grin.

He shook his head. "You're amazing, you know that? To look at you, no one would guess that you eat so much."

"Appearances are deceiving." She took a sip of the tall glass of milk she'd ordered with her meal and dabbed at her lips with the napkin.

Bryce wondered if she was doing it on purpose, drawing his attention to the kissable curve of her mouth. Not that such a ruse would be necessary; he was already finding it difficult to keep his thoughts, let alone his hands, off her.

Lisa began eating her pie. "As soon as we're done here," she was saying, "we can go back and pick up the rocking horse. The dealer was going to wrap it for me so it won't get damaged during the trip home, but he should be done with that by now."

Bryce promptly reached for the bill, which sat in that neutral zone between the salt and the pepper shakers. "I'll take care of lunch."

"No, you won't." She tried to tug the bill away from him. "We'll go dutch."

"No." Bryce tugged it back out of her grasp. "It's my treat. Consider it payment for your brief history lesson on the gold rush days."

"I don't require payment," she retorted heatedly.

"Okay, maybe that was a bad choice of words. Perhaps equal exchange would have been a better term to use.

What's the big deal about my springing for lunch? A couple of dollars isn't exactly going to break me, you know."

"I don't like being beholden to anyone."

Bryce could tell by the look in her eye that she was talking about more than a simple lunch bill here. More pieces of the puzzle. Someone or something had made this a sore point with her. Seeing how defensive she was, he relented for the moment. "All right, we'll go dutch. But I leave the tip."

She flashed him a smile that was almost grateful. "Fine."

They walked from the restaurant to the toy store in companionable silence.

As they neared the store, Bryce spoke first. "Is it my imagination, or do I hear water running?" he asked with a quizzical lift of one eyebrow.

"Amador Creek runs behind these buildings."

"Does it have gold in it?"

"Probably. Traces, at least." The same way his hair had traces of gold in it as the sun beat down on them, she noted. And how had he learned to lift one eyebrow and not the other? It softened his classical features, making him look more accessible and even better looking—though he was already too attractive for her peace of mind. And she didn't want him staring at her that way, with a mixture of attraction and interest that bordered on desire. Okay, so it *was* desire. Why should it matter to her if he desired her?

It didn't matter, she quickly assured herself. He was looking at her that way only because he thought she was after his grandmother's fortune. He wanted to charm her into leaving Ellie, and her money, alone.

Still, she had to admit that he was disturbing her peace of mind, not to mention her concentration. What had she been talking about before? Ah, yes, gold.

"Did I tell you that gold was first discovered in this area in 1848?"

"You did mention that, yes," he noted in amusement.

"Oh. Nice wisteria, huh?" She pointed to the clusters of purple flowers hanging from a trellis on the toy store's porch.

"Beautiful," he murmured, but he wasn't looking at the flowers. He was looking at her. And getting to her.

Lisa frowned and forced her eyes away from his. What was wrong with her? She wasn't normally the kind who flustered easily.

She was still trying to pull herself together when Bryce reached out and brushed his fingers against her cheek. Startled, she took a step backward and almost skewered herself on the wooden trellis.

Brilliant move, Lisa, she congratulated herself. Angered by her sudden bout of clumsiness, Lisa attempted to move away, but some of the shrub's branches were caught in her hair.

"Here." He came closer. "Let me help you."

You're the reason I'm in this mess, she thought. But she stood still, her eyes daring him to take advantage of her temporary immobility.

The smile on his face made her suspicious, but other than taking his time about freeing her, he didn't make any obvious moves. There were a few occasions when she could have sworn that she felt his fingers caress the tip of her ear, the nape of her neck, but he met her distrustful glares with a look so innocent that she decided she'd been mistaken. It must have been the wisteria blossoms brushing against her skin. Or maybe it had just been her imagination.

"There you go. Free again."

She wanted to make some snappy comeback, but all she could come up with was "Thank you."

"You're welcome."

Lisa resolutely blocked the incident from her mind the moment she entered the toy dealer's store. Instead, she firmly kept her thoughts on the transportation of the rocking horse.

"Are you sure that will fit in your car?" Bryce asked doubtfully.

"Positive."

A few minutes later, as they stood next to the VW, she said, "Okay, so I was wrong!" The rocking horse had proved to be an inch too long.

"It will fit in the back seat of my car." Bryce held open the Buick's large back door invitingly. "What's the matter?" he asked as she hesitated. "Afraid I'll kidnap your rocking horse?"

"No, it's not fancy enough for your tastes."

Bryce shook his head. "We really are going to have to discuss these misconceptions you have about me. But for now, let's get this baby loaded."

As she drove back to Jamestown, with Bryce and the rocking horse following, Lisa brooded. Remembering how he'd brushed his fingers against her cheek, she raised one hand to her face as if expecting the warmth of his touch to still be there. A moment later she chastised herself for the romantic gesture. Daydreaming about some things was fine, but daydreaming about Bryce was not.

By the time Lisa brought her VW to a halt in front of her house, she'd managed to put the incident back into its proper prospective. She had other things to think about. As Bryce parked behind her, she could imagine how the place looked through his eyes. Why hadn't she noticed before that the Christmas lights were still up from last December? The grass in the front yard needed watering, and the front porch could have used a new coat of paint. It might not be much, but the small rental was her home. What did she care what he thought, anyway?

Bryce could tell from Lisa's defensive stance that she was just waiting for him to make some disparaging comment. But all he said was "Where do you want me to put the rocking horse?"

"Inside. Be careful." she said as he tugged it out of the car. "Treat it gently."

He turned to look at her with the wooden rocking horse in his arms. "I can be very gentle," he noted in a voice that was rich with intimacy and promise.

Good, she wanted to tell him. *Then direct that attention to the horse and not me.* But that would be admitting that his attention disturbed her, so she acted as if he didn't bother her, and she made sure to stand firm when he brushed past her as she held open the screen door.

Bryce nudged the door a little further so both he and his burden could fit. Once inside the house, he looked around the living room with more than casual curiosity, seeking clues to Lisa's personality. She was unconventional, and he saw that her home was, too. The only normal piece of living room furniture she owned was a couch. A pastel horse from a merry-go-round occupied the space normally reserved for an end table. The tables she did have looked like chunks of trees—polished and oiled but giving the impression that they'd just mushroomed out of the hardwood floor. There were lots of plants scattered around, and a colorful array of pottery. Three enlarged photographs graced the otherwise bare walls.

While there weren't many furnishings, the room was far from austere. The floor had been treated with a dark wood stain, and the walls had been painted pale peach.

Noting his interest, she said, "The landlord told me I could paint the place any color I wanted, so I did."

As far as Bryce was concerned, the color scheme suited her. Fresh, not harsh. He liked it and he told her so.

Because she'd been nervously waiting for his reaction, she hid her feelings beneath a layer of mocking humor. "Thanks for your approval, counselor."

"It is small, though," he noted as he looked around for someplace to put the bulky rocking horse.

"I prefer to call it cozy."

"Are you sure you want to keep this thing here and not at my grandmother's house? It doesn't look like you have enough room to be storing something this big. And God knows there's enough room in her house for a hundred rocking horses."

"I know. Those old Victorians are wonderful, aren't they? So roomy, with little nooks and crannies everywhere. But this particular rocking horse is a surprise for Ellie. I want to get it cleaned up before I show it to her. Here, there's room in this corner. Put it here."

When he did, she said, "Thanks for carrying it in for me." She then felt obligated to repay him with the offer of a cup of coffee.

He accepted and followed her into the kitchen.

As she reached into a cabinet for two coffee mugs, she was very much aware of his eyes on her. She took a calming breath before asking, "Do you take your coffee black or with cream and sugar?"

"Cream, no sugar." He watched as she set the mugs on the counter. A few minutes later, he noted, "Do you realize that we've actually gone all afternoon without having an argument?"

"Hard to believe, isn't it?"

"I think it proves a point."

"Which is?"

"That we have more in common than you think."

"Like what?"

"We both like our coffee with cream and no sugar," he pointed out.

"Yes, but I'll bet you're used to your coffee being served in fine china, while I'm used to drinking it from a Styrofoam cup or, at best, a mug."

"Ah, the clash of the classes again, right? You know, I find it interesting that you're a lot more concerned about the differences in our backgrounds than I am," he remarked.

"I'm not concerned."

"No? What would you call it, then?"

"Being prudent."

"Now, there's a thought. You being prudent." Bryce shook his head. "Somehow I find it hard seeing you that way."

"I can be very prudent if the situation warrants it."

"I make you feel prudent? I have to confess, it's not the effect I have on most women."

"I'm not most women."

"I know."

Lisa recognized the look he gave her. It was warm and intimate, intended to make her feel special, and it did. If only it were real.

"You didn't answer my first question," he softly reminded her. "Why do you feel you have to be prudent with me?"

"Maybe it has something to do with the way you barged into the store yesterday and accused me of trying to embezzle money from your grandmother, but, hey... maybe I'm just being sensitive."

"That must be it," Bryce agreed with a straight face. "You're just being overly sensitive and needlessly prudent. I'll have to see what I can do to change that."

"You could try not looking at me as if you suspected I might take off with the family silver," she suggested.

"If that's the way you think I've been looking at you, then my technique must be slipping."

Lisa and Bryce gazed at each other, and suddenly they were doing more than just sharing a cup of coffee. It came as something of a surprise to her to realize that in just one day they'd already shared laughter, conversation, anger, information, and plenty of sexy looks—not to mention that little incident with the wisteria bush. She wondered where this was all leading. Nowhere, she reminded herself firmly. Nowhere at all.

Although she tried not to show it, she could feel herself tensing up, as if anticipating Bryce's next move. When he left shortly thereafter without so much as a polite handshake, she told herself she wasn't disappointed. He'd smiled nicely enough, thanked her for the coffee and made his departure.

She closed the door after him. She told herself that she should be feeling relieved now that he was gone, but her emotions were more complicated than that. She liked him, she didn't like him. She was attracted to him, she wasn't attracted to him.

She was still standing there, by the door when someone knocked on it. Surprised, she turned around and opened it.

Bryce stood there. "I forgot something," he said in a courteous, and slightly apologetic, tone of voice.

She took a step back as she automatically looked around for something he might have left behind. "You did? What?"

"This." He framed her face with his hands and leaned forward to kiss her.

He caught her by surprise. It wasn't just the kiss; it was the *way* he kissed her. His lips brushed hers with a light caress that was there and gone, a gentle prelude for what was yet to come. It was as if she and Bryce were feeling their way, all the while looking into each other's eyes, reading the doubt, the confusion, and finally...the need written there.

Overwhelmed, Lisa closed her eyes. The warm taste of his mouth erased all her reservations as he pulled her closer. Now the kiss developed into something more, something warm and seductive. His lips became bolder, and her response was equally fervent. What had started as a sweet temptation had rapidly escalated into an enticing hunger swirling around them, drawing them in.

She panicked and pulled away. Suddenly this situation with Bryce was no longer a laughing matter. She was definitely in trouble here.

Four

———

"You seem awfully quiet, Lisa. Is something wrong?" Ellie asked her the next morning. The two of them were in The Toy Chest, compiling a list of possible donors for the toy museum.

"Nothing's wrong," Lisa replied.

"No?" Ellie pointed to the notepad Lisa had been working on. "Then why have you written down the same name three times in a row?"

Lisa crossed off the duplications. "Sorry about that. I guess I'm a little tired. I didn't sleep very well last night."

"It's Bryce, isn't it?"

"What makes you think Bryce had anything to do with it?"

"Because I know him and I know you. And while I love Bryce dearly, he can be annoyingly stubborn sometimes. He told me he spent the day with you yesterday. Did you two fight again?"

"Not really. Actually, he was on his best behavior."

"Good. I don't want him bothering you."

It was too late for that, Lisa knew. He already had bothered her—badly. She couldn't get their kiss out of her mind. Telling herself that he'd caught her by surprise simply didn't cut the ice any longer. She'd enjoyed the kiss and been an equal partner in it; there was no getting around that fact.

Which left her where? she asked herself. Confused, was the first answer that came to mind. And what had she learned from the experience? That Bryce was dangerous to her peace of mind. That he could turn a kiss into a gentle seduction that melted her resistance along with most of her backbone. It had been an alarming discovery, to put it mildly. No wonder she'd been up half the night brooding about it.

And what about Bryce? She thought he'd looked equally stunned after kissing her, but she couldn't be sure. He hadn't said a word to her when he'd left. But he had given her a smile that really had her worried. Not only had it been an honest-to-God genuine smile, one that had been reflected in his blue eyes, but it had told her things she didn't want to know, conveyed promises she didn't want him to keep.

"I can tell something is wrong. Do you feel like talking about it?" Ellie asked with maternal concern.

Lisa nodded, knowing that she'd need help regrouping her defenses against Bryce's charm. But first she had something she wanted to clear up. "Ellie, are you sure you wouldn't rather work with someone else on the toy museum? I don't want you to feel obligated to continue having me on this project if it's going to create problems between you and your family. Maybe you'd be better off with someone else in charge."

"Nonsense." Ellie gave her a reassuring hug. "We make an excellent team. Don't let Bryce upset you."

"Easier said than done, I'm afraid."

"What's he done?"

"Nothing really. He's being very nice to me. *Too* nice," she said with a disapproving frown. "He's trying to charm me."

"And is he succeeding?"

"Of course not. I know what his game is. He's only sweet-talking me so that he can get rid of me. He wants me to trust him, and when I do, he'll pull the rug out from under me. All he really wants is for me to be out of your life."

"I'm not sure that's *all* he wants," Ellie replied. "He seemed awfully preoccupied this morning. He's asked me questions about you for the past two days, and now suddenly he says nothing. I can't figure it out."

"He's probably planning his next mode of attack. Is he still determined to spend the next two weeks here?"

Ellie nodded. "The more I try to convince him not to, the more determined he becomes, so I've given up that approach. It obviously isn't going to work. But I know Bryce. He's a workaholic. All this peace and quiet is going to drive him to distraction sooner or later. He's going to miss his office, his business conferences."

"And if he doesn't?" Lisa asked.

"Then he'll be here for the two weeks." Ellie sighed. "I'm sorry about all of this. I never meant to draw you into a family squabble."

"It's not your fault." It was Lisa's turn to hug Ellie. "If Harold were less paranoid, if I were less unconventional— maybe this wouldn't have happened."

"Harold wouldn't trust whomever I put in charge of the museum. He's always guarded the family wealth very jealously. If he'd had his way, I wouldn't have gotten a penny of what he considers Stephenson money. But Samuel left the money to me, so there's not much Harold can do. I'm sure it irks Harold even more to think Stephenson money is being used for something as frivolous as a toy museum. There's no way to make a profit at it, which is Harold's top criterion for any action. Even Bryce thinks it's silly, although he hasn't said so, yet.''

"He's already asked me what qualifications I have to take on a project like the toy museum,'' Lisa admitted.

Ellie shook her head. "I really am going to have to have a word with that boy. I've told him that I'm perfectly capable of making my own decisions, but he says that he's worried about me. I've told him that I trust you implicitly and that should be enough for him. Obviously it isn't, but that's no reason to keep harassing you.''

"Well, if he's going to be around for the next two weeks, I'm just going to have to learn how to deal with it.''

"You've been doing wonderfully so far. I've never seen Bryce so...confused before. Normally he's completely in control. But I get the definite impression that you intrigue him.''

"It's not intentional, believe me. I've got no desire to get tangled up with him or with his wealthy family's paranoia.''

Lisa's vehement declaration made Ellie say, "This is bringing back memories of your marriage, isn't it?''

Lisa nodded. "And I have to admit that they're not very pleasant memories. But then, as you know, my marriage to David wasn't a very pleasant experience. Strange how eight months can change your life. That's all it was, you know. Eight months. Then it was over. I'll never forget coming home from work and finding David's father waiting for me.'' She paused as the hurtful words came back to haunt her. "The man was very blunt about it. He told me that

David regretted having married me and wanted it ended. I didn't believe him at first, but when David later confirmed it . . ." She shook her head and looked away. "I felt guilty accepting the settlement money at first, but then I had been supporting David on my salary for most of our married life. He'd never been able to hold on to a job for very long. So, as David's parents would say, I took the money and ran."

"And you used that money to help pay for your father's hospital bills. He told me about that." Ellie patted Lisa's hand. "Your marriage may have been brief, but it's left scars. I know that."

Lisa nodded. "I guess we both know what it feels like to be thought of as inferior in some way. It isn't very pleasant." Her voice became lighter as she added, "But back to the matter at hand. Bryce's charm. Maybe we should try ignoring him—what do you think?"

"We could try it, but it might just make him more determined."

"Well, we've already ruled out telling him to butt out, because that would make him more determined. What *will* work? Avoiding him?"

"No. I think we should just act natural and let Bryce know that nothing he can do will dissuade us," Ellie said.

Personally Lisa preferred the idea of avoiding Bryce, but when he walked into the store later that afternoon, she realized how hopeless that would be. Jamestown was small, and Bryce was definitely on her trail.

The first thing he did was look at her mouth, as if remembering the taste of her. Actually, she thought he was more than just looking; he was staring, eating her up with his eyes. She tried to keep her cool by turning her back on him and concentrating on rearranging an array of plush animals on a glass shelf behind the counter. Now she felt his gaze on her back. A few seconds later she felt his fingers slide down her spine in a teasing caress.

She gulped and quickly turned around. "Don't do that!"

"Do what?"

"You know what. Don't touch me like that."

"Bothers you, does it?"

"Damn right." She regretted the admission as soon as she'd made it. She'd given him the advantage, and he was making the most of it, eyeing her the way a hunter eyes its prey. But she could still turn this situation around. She just needed to figure out how.

"You didn't seem to mind when I kissed you last night," he murmured confidently.

His comment restored her sense of purpose. He was just waiting for her to deny it, to get angry again. But she was back in control now, and she planned on staying that way. "It was a nice enough kiss...."

"Nice?" He looked insulted.

"But that was last night and this is today. I've got a lot of work to get done. We're beginning inventory in a few days, and I don't have the time for fooling around. You may be on vacation, but I'm not." Her voice was now pleasantly cheerful, and she could see that it threw him.

"You're not going to get rid of me that quickly."

"I know that."

"If you're busy now, then come out to dinner with me tonight and we'll talk then."

"Fine. Pick me up at seven."

He raised an eyebrow in surprise. "You're accepting?"

"Yes. Wasn't I supposed to?"

"Yes, but why do I get the impression you're up to something?"

She shrugged. "Must be natural paranoia on your part. Where are we going for dinner?"

"I've heard that the Jamestown Hotel has an excellent dining room."

"You heard right. A good choice." Lisa smiled. She knew most of the people who worked there; she wouldn't be facing Bryce alone. "See you at seven, then."

"Fine. And just so you know, we're not going dutch tonight." Bryce would have said more, but a boisterous group entered the store. "We'll talk tonight," he promised.

"Sure. We'll talk some more about Jamestown's history."

"That's not necessary."

"Nonsense. It's the least I can do for the grandson of a good friend of mine."

"The least? What's the most?"

"Let me rephrase that. It's the *only* thing I'll do for the grandson of a good friend of mine."

"Don't make promises you can't keep, Lisa," he said softly.

Right, Lisa, she told herself after he'd left. Watch out for those promises. And while you're at it, watch out for Bryce. The man was definitely a threat to her peace of mind, a peace of mind that was further disturbed by a customer's exclamation.

"Mommy said not to put your fingers on that! Stop it right now!"

Lisa had to hurry over to save a display from certain disaster. Her day was unusually busy, with customers coming in and out at a steady rate. By the time she locked up at six she was ready to put her feet up and read a good book. Instead, she had to get ready to face Bryce. The prospect required all her strength and composure.

A quick shower restored most of her optimism, and now, as she stood in front of her dresser mirror, she felt confident about her choice of outfit. The white dress, demurely trimmed with eyelet, was a throwback to another era—an era of modestly scooped necklines and long hemlines. She left her dark hair loose and wore no jewelry other than a watch.

She didn't think that the innocent look would appeal to a man like Bryce. The moment she opened the door and saw the way he was looking at her, she discovered she was wrong. He liked what he saw.

She was doing some looking herself—at him. She, too, liked what she saw. He was wearing dark slacks, a blue shirt and a sports jacket. As always he exuded good taste, but tonight there was something different about him. His clothing was as well tailored as ever, although his hair was slightly ruffled.

What was it about him that made him seem even more attractive than he had before? she wondered. Was it the lack of suspicion in his gaze? Or was it the slight curve of his lips as he restrained a smile instead of flashing it? Even his hello sounded quietly unsteady instead of confidently charming. His entire attitude seemed changed. Or was that part of his plan?

This was crazy. She was analyzing every little thing. She must be getting lightheaded from lack of food. She'd skipped lunch again today. The explanation made her feel better. Finally realizing that she'd kept Bryce standing on her doorstep, she hastily stepped aside.

"Come on in. I'll be ready in a minute," she said.

I'm ready now, Bryce was thinking. Ready to make love to her. Desire had hit him with the suddenness of a blow. One look at her and he was hot and heavy. He shifted restlessly. It was that dress. It was white and should have made her look as innocent as an angel. Instead she only looked incredibly sexy. Her dark, wavy hair fell around her shoulders in glorious abandon. He wanted to sweep her off her feet and take her to bed. But it was too soon.

Summoning up his willpower, Bryce stepped inside and pretended a polite interest in the photographs on her living room wall. Needing the break to recover his self-control, he kept his eyes on the photographs and away from Lisa.

"These are nice," he said when she came and stood by his side. "Did you take them?"

Lisa shook her head. "No, a friend did. She specializes in photographs of Yosemite. I tell her she's the next Ansel Adams."

"I've got an Ansel Adams print on my office wall in Chicago. The man had a genius for blending light and dark, black and white, and creating magic."

"He certainly did. Which print do you have?"

"You know, I can't remember exactly what it looks like...."

His answer disappointed her. Here she'd been thinking that they might have something in common, however small, and it turned out to be just an illusion. "The print was probably chosen by your interior decorator because it matched your decor, right?"

"No, I chose it myself. I even hung it myself. I look at it all the time. I've just been so busy lately I haven't had the time to see it."

"You mean you usually walk around in a daze, so wrapped up in your work that you don't notice anything else? Somehow that doesn't surprise me."

It surprised him, he reflected. Maybe he needed this break from the office more than he'd realized. He still couldn't believe he hadn't been able to describe the print. Normally his memory was infallible. But then he hadn't been feeling normal since he'd met Lisa; he supposed there was no reason for that to change now.

"I made a reservation for seven-thirty." Bryce checked his watch. "If we leave now, we'll have just enough time to walk there."

"Spoken like a man who follows a strict timetable."

He nodded and held the front door open for her. "And you sound like a woman who dislikes schedules."

"I admit that I like to take the time to stop and smell the roses along the way." She paused on the sidewalk. "There, can you smell it?"

"Smell what?"

"Fresh air, pine trees and just a hint of lilac blossoms."

Once again Bryce was struck by the way she enjoyed the small things—details that most people never even noticed, himself included. If he was ever going to unravel Lisa's mysteries and figure her out, he'd have to pay more attention to the details concerning her life. He hoped he'd learn more about her over dinner this evening.

The hotel's dining room was crowded. Bryce soon discovered why. Not only were the restored Victorian surroundings charming, but the food was delicious. The conversation wasn't bad, either.

As promised, Lisa spent the better part of the meal telling him about Jamestown's colorful history.

"Did I tell you that the town's founding father was a lawyer?" she asked. When Bryce shook his head, she went on. "Colonel George James was a San Francisco attorney who tried his luck here and founded the town. He didn't stick around very long afterward, though. The story is that he fought with the other miners and ended up leaving."

"And I suppose you're going to tell me that the moral to the story is that lawyers who come to town shouldn't start fights."

"Right."

"I'll keep it in mind." But what he actually kept in mind was the sight of Lisa daintily licking the last of the cheesecake from her fork. Her lips, her tongue... He groaned. Even having her talk about the gold rush was preferable to being driven crazy this way. At least while so many people were around, all of whom seemed to know Lisa. "Tell me more," he prompted her.

"In those days the town became affectionately known as Jimtown," she said, then went on to tell him a few amusing stories from the town's colorful past.

"You said you got your love for that period in history from your parents. How long have they had gold fever?"

"Since their first visit here."

"Which was when?" he asked.

"Back in the late sixties, I think."

"They've lived here ever since?"

"No, they were only visiting at the time. We did that a lot in the summers. Just pack up the car and take off. My parents treated a trip to California as if it were an afternoon's drive, even though we were living in Ohio at the time." She smiled and took a sip of her Irish coffee. "We were always having great adventures, doing things on the spur of the moment."

Bryce refused to get frustrated by her artful dodging. She was answering his questions without really telling him anything. Patience was a virtue he'd always possessed in the past; it was time to put it to use now. "It sounds like you and your parents have a good relationship."

She nodded.

"It must be nice having them live close by."

She nodded again.

"Do you get to see them very often?"

Another nod.

"Want to lend me fifty dollars?"

She blinked. "What?!"

"Just checking to see if you were paying attention. You were nodding so much I couldn't tell."

"I always pay attention. Do you?"

"Why? Is there going to be a quiz? Want me to repeat the early episodes of life in Jimtown? I know Colonel James came here for gold, but I want to know why you came here. To be near your parents?"

"Partially."

"And the other part?"

"I like it here."

"You've stayed here longer than you have in most places. Why?"

"Why have I stayed, or why have I moved around so much?"

"Both."

"When I was growing up, my parents were always intrigued by what was over the next hill. I guess I inherited some of that curiosity. I've been in Jamestown for almost three years now and I haven't felt that tug to go somewhere else since I got here."

She'd expected him to make some sarcastic comment about her staying because of Ellie, but he didn't bring up his grandmother's name at all. She pondered on that fact as Bryce walked her home. Did he still think she was after Ellie's money? Was this evening just another attempt to get her to slip up, to make some unintentional comment that would confirm his opinion of her?

He hadn't seemed to mind that she'd spent so much of the evening talking about Jamestown and only a small portion talking about herself. But then he was clever. He knew that pushing her would only make her more determined not to tell him anything. She supposed that was something they both had in common; they were both the type to dig in their heels when pushed.

The walk back to her house seemed shorter than the walk to the hotel had been. She'd left the front porch light on, which meant the Christmas lights were also on.

"I've been meaning to do something about those lights," she murmured with a shake of her head.

"And I've been meaning to do this...." A gentle tug and she was in his arms. A moment later his lips were on hers, coaxing them apart. At the first touch of his tongue, she was lost.

She forgot that they were standing on her front porch, spotlighted by the porch light, clearly visible to any passersby. She forgot her newfound resolution to fight Bryce's charm. She forgot everything except the memory of how perfectly their mouths blended together. There was no awkwardness, only excitement and pleasure. Without considering the consequences, Lisa allowed her eyes to close and her lips to part.

Bryce immediately intensified the kiss, deepening the pressure of his mouth on hers until the kiss became a heated seduction. Pulling her closer, he ran his fingers through her hair before cupping the back of her head in his hands.

One kiss blended into the next, punctuated by tiny nibbles and husky sighs. When Lisa shyly touched the tip of her tongue to his bottom lip, Bryce responded by boldly greeting her tongue with his. The ensuing interplay was so incredibly erotic that she melted against him.

Lisa heard his triumphant growl, felt it as he gathered her even closer to him. She knew what it meant. He thought he'd won while she'd abandoned the fight. But she couldn't afford to surrender. He could end up with a huge chunk of her heart if she let him. And she'd end up with nothing but heartache.

Warning bells went off in her head. She had to protect herself. Although dazed by the passion he'd aroused in her, Lisa knew she had to break away, while she still could.

Her sudden retreat surprised Bryce. He reached for her again, but she put out her hands in a defensive gesture meant to discourage him.

"Look, this just isn't going to work." Her bold declaration sounded weak and unsteady even to her own ears.

Bryce stealthily moved closer. "What isn't?" he murmured, sliding his arms around her waist and pulling her to him.

"You charming me."

"How about my seducing you?" He nuzzled her neck.

For one brief moment she melted before shying away. "That won't work, either."

"Why not?"

"Because I know why you're doing this!" The words gave her the strength to move away from him completely, putting several feet between them.

"You do?"

"Yes. You're doing it because you want me to leave your grandmother, and more importantly, her money, alone. You're hoping to romance me into confessing that I'm some sort of thief."

"I don't think you're a thief."

"You don't *think*, but you're not *sure*."

"Stop putting words in my mouth. You're complicating something that's really quite simple."

"Sure." She began pacing. "And I suppose you're going to tell me that you only kissed me because you want me and not for any other reason."

His smile looked whimsical in the soft light. "I would have stated it a bit more romantically than that, but that's the gist of it, yes."

"Why should I believe you?"

"Why shouldn't you?"

"Because less than a week ago you walked in here and tried to buy me off, accusing me of stealing money from your grandmother."

He took hold of her hand, stopping her restless pacing. "I didn't know you then."

She tugged her hand away. "You don't know me now."

"Not as well as I'd like to, but I know enough about you. You're unconventional, yes, but basically not dishonest."

She was miffed. "What do you mean *basically* not dishonest?"

"You're only dishonest if you deny what's between us."

"Oh, really? And what *is* between us?"

"This." He leaned down and softly kissed her, a bare brushing of lips that was there and then gone. But the feelings remained. He gazed into her eyes, daring her to look away. "We've got something special going for us. I know it, and so do you."

"It's called chemistry," she whispered huskily, unable to tear her eyes away from his.

"Call it what you will. It's something we both feel and something we both want to explore."

She wanted to explore him, all right. She wanted to unbutton his shirt and run her hands over his bare skin. She wanted to explore that stubborn strength of his jaw with the tip of her tongue. She wanted to explore the passion she saw in his eyes.

As if able to read her thoughts, Bryce gently tugged her into his arms. This time his kiss was warm and tender, filled with meanings she couldn't interpret. There was a caring, a yearning, a hunger that seemed to find a matching emotion within her. It was as if his heart spoke directly to hers, bypassing the mind. Her heart answered. So did her lips. Softly, sensually, she kissed him back.

His embrace gradually tightened until she could feel everything about him—his jacket buttons pressing against her dress, the warmth of his chest through the thin material of his shirt, the stirring strength of his arousal.

She savored the heady newness of it all. One kiss developed into another as their lips touched, parted and touched again.

"Tell me what you want," he murmured against her mouth.

"For you to believe in me." She pulled away as if regretting the words as soon as she'd said them.

"Now what's wrong?" he asked.

"You're making me care," she practically wailed.

He smoothed his hand across her cheek. "What's wrong with that?"

"Everything." She took a step backward. "It doesn't change anything. You can't come out to California thinking I'm some kind of thief and then suddenly turn around and expect me to go to bed with you."

"I haven't even asked you, yet."

"You ask me every time you kiss me."

He smiled. "You noticed that, did you?"

"I noticed. Surely you can see that I'm going to be skeptical of your motives."

"Just as I was skeptical of yours until I met you. Then certain things didn't fit. You certainly didn't react like someone who was guilty. In fact, you laughed in my face."

"I didn't actually laugh."

"You were amused."

"Maybe I was just being clever."

"And maybe you were just being honest."

"That's a distinct possibility, I suppose."

"Come on. Why is it so hard for you to admit that we're attracted to each other?"

"Even if we are, that doesn't change anything. You're still who you are and I'm still who I am."

"I like who you are."

His words went right to her heart. She couldn't say a thing.

"And I know that you'd never hurt my grandmother," he added.

"What convinced you of that?"

"*You* convinced me of that. Now I have to convince you. I know it won't be easy. You've been hurt in the past. I know that you were married briefly and that it didn't work out."

"Oh, you can be more specific than that. I was briefly married to a man who came from a very wealthy family, a family that ended up paying me to get out of their son's life. That's what your investigator's report said, right? Aren't you afraid of getting tangled up with a gold digger?"

"Lady, I'd love to get tangled up with you. Unfortunately, you won't let me. And you're no more a gold digger than I am. You're not going to be able to hide behind that smoke screen much longer." His hand cupped her obstinate chin as he ran his thumb along her jawline. "Sooner or later you're going to have to face the fact that there *is* something between us. Just be warned that I plan on doing everything I can to make sure you face it sooner, rather than later!" He kissed her one last time. "Sleep on it. I'll see you in the morning."

Five

Lisa had to get away. She needed a break from Bryce's attention. She couldn't think clearly anymore. Maybe distance would give her some much-needed objectivity. At least she hoped so.

As soon as she got up the next morning she made arrangements to take a short trip to Nevada City. The trip would accomplish several things: she could check on the Victorian Museum there and get ideas for the toy museum; she could visit her parents, who were prospecting in that area; and she could get away from Bryce—even if it was only for a day or two.

Just having made that decision made her feel better. Unfortunately, she wouldn't be able to leave until noon, when her assistant, Judy, came in. To keep herself busy, Lisa began a preliminary inventory. She knew she was running the risk of Bryce showing up before she went away, but there was nothing she could do about it—except to expect him and be prepared. So she did just that.

She'd almost finished counting the number of windup ladybugs on the shelf when Bryce walked in. She held up a hand requesting silence as she continued counting. "Twenty-three, twenty-four, twenty-five, twenty-six! Finally!" She jotted down the number on her clipboard. "I've already counted these things twice." She was rather pleased with how calm and impersonal she sounded. Actually, she was afraid that Bryce was going to make some reference to their kiss last night, but instead he frowned at her clipboard.

"A computerized inventory and register system would eliminate the need for this kind of counting," he said. "It went out with the dark ages, along with that huge monstrosity you call a cash register. Think how much more efficient an automated system would be. You could maintain inventory records, calculate sales tax and figure the change to be returned to the customer all at the press of a button."

Lisa didn't know whether to be relieved or insulted that he was calmly discussing business matters. She only knew that she was getting more and more aggravated by the minute. "It might be more efficient, but it would lack originality. The register I have has character, and our stock isn't large enough yet that we can't do our inventory manually. Besides," she said defensively, "since when have you been an expert on retailing?"

"It doesn't take an expert to see where improvement is needed."

"I'll tell you what needs improving. Your attitude. You can't just walk into a place and start telling people how to run their lives, or their businesses!"

Realizing her outburst was somewhat out of proportion to this comments, Lisa paused to regroup. She'd been able to stay calm for, what, maybe five minutes in his presence. Not a very impressive record, she told herself. Keep your cool, and keep things on an impersonal level.

"We're not ready yet for automation," she stated firmly. "And the antique register fits in with the locale. Around here, we value history."

"If that's the way you feel about it, I only have one more thing to say."

"Which is?" She crossed her arms in a militant fashion, preparing herself for battle.

"You have a smudge of dirt on your chin."

That was the last thing she expected him to say. Frowning, she quickly attempted to rub away any possible smudge. However, since she couldn't see what she was doing, she wasn't sure if she was improving things or not.

"No, you're just making it worse. Here, allow me." He reached beyond her to pull a facial tissue from the box on the counter. Holding her chin between his fingers, he tilted her face up to his. Then he gently rubbed the tissue across her smooth skin. "There. Much better." He brushed his fingers across her now smudge-free skin. "Have dinner with me tonight."

"I can't. I've got other plans."

Something in her eyes made him suspicious. "Not thinking of running away, are you?" Her guilty start told him that he'd guessed correctly. "Okay, what are you up to?"

"Twenty-six windup ladybugs. Next I start counting the plastic dinosaurs."

"All right." He shrugged amiably. "Don't tell me. I'll find out anyway. I'll just keep following you until you do tell me."

"In that case you could be here awhile. And that being true, I might as well put you to work." She handed him the clipboard. "You can start by counting the plastic dinosaurs."

To her surprise, he did as she requested, even though she knew it had sounded more like an order than a request. She'd done that deliberately, hoping he'd get angry and leave. But now she was glad that he hadn't.

Her feelings were bouncing up and down more than the yo-yos she was currently counting. And Bryce was holding the string. A flick of his wrist and he had her dangling in midair; another move and she was held secure in the palm of his hand.

Bryce glanced over and wondered why Lisa was staring so intently at a yo-yo. "Something wrong?" he asked her.

She blinked in surprise. "No. Umm, I was just thinking."

He knew Lisa well enough by now to realize that she wouldn't tell him any more unless she wanted him to know. So he made some noncommittal reply and began counting. Every other dinosaur, he paused and watched Lisa.

To see her was to want her. He saw the sun shining down on her hair, and he wanted to touch her as the sun was touching her—freely. She fascinated him. The curve of her lips, her shoulders, her breasts. She was all curves. And all fire. Her dark hair shone with hidden light; her eyes flashed and sparkled.

"Stop that," she said in a husky voice.

"Stop what?"

"You're staring at me."

"I know. I can't help it."

And she couldn't help responding to those looks he gave her. Her breath caught in her throat and she couldn't think clearly. *Exactly,* a voice inside her head shouted. *This is why you have to get away from him for a while.*

As if he'd read her mind, he softly said, "I *will* follow you, you know."

"Why? I'll be back tomorrow afternoon."

"Where are you going?"

"Nevada City. And you don't want to come along."

"I know. Your VW is too small, and besides that, I distract you."

"I never said that. About your distracting me, I mean."

"You didn't have to say it."

"Concentrate on those dinosaurs, would you please? This inventory count has to be accurate."

"Yes, ma'am," he drawled.

She wanted to plunk a Stetson on his head and see how he'd look as a cowboy. She wanted to kiss him senseless. She wanted to believe that his attention had nothing to do with his grandmother.

She didn't know what to do. She didn't want him following her to Nevada City. And she wouldn't put it past him to do just that. She'd rather have him beside her, where she could keep an eye on him, than have him behind her, where she didn't know what he was up to. She suspected he felt the same about her. But then she suspected a lot of things and wasn't sure of any of them.

So at noon, after Judy had taken over at the store, Lisa walked outside and turned to face Bryce, who was right behind her.

"All right, already. You can come along! We'll be gone overnight, though. You might want to bring a change of clothes along."

"Good idea. I'll pick you up at your place in fifteen minutes," he said, looking very pleased with himself.

But Lisa still had a few surprises up her sleeve. Bryce wasn't going to find everything going his way. And he was going to be in for more than he'd bargained for.

They drove northward along route 49 again, passing Amador City. Lisa couldn't believe how much things had changed since the afternoon they'd stopped there. Bryce had kissed her, told her that he trusted her and that he didn't believe she was out to hurt Ellie.

Could she believe him? Did she want to? The answer to that last question was yes. She was still brooding about the answer to the first question when Bryce asked her a question of his own.

"Why toys?"

"What?"

"Why this interest of yours in toys?"

"I guess it started with Oscar."

"Who's Oscar?" he asked suspiciously.

"My first teddy bear. I still have him, despite all the moving we did. Even though I've added quite a few more teddy bears to my collection, Oscar will always have a special place in my heart."

She glanced over at Bryce, who looked thoughtful. "Tell me something. Have you ever had a teddy bear?"

"No. What's that got to do with anything?"

"What kind of toys *did* you have as a kid?"

Bryce paused, suddenly remembering how as an eight-year-old he'd desperately wanted a set of small racing cars for Christmas. Instead, he'd gotten blue-chip stock certificates. They'd been more practical in the long run. Still... He shook his head, banishing the moment of regret. "I had a few educational toys."

She made a face.

"I'd prefer a warm, cuddly teddy bear to a supposedly educational toy any day. Besides, teddy bears *are* educational. They teach you a lot about yourself."

"I find that hard to believe."

"It's true. Sometimes people feel freer talking to a non-threatening teddy bear than to another human being. That's why some doctors use them with their patients. And police officers in squad cars use teddy bears to reassure scared kids."

"Where did you hear that?"

"I read it in a teddy bear magazine. Why? Did you think I was speaking from my own personal experience in the back of a police squad car?"

He shook his head. "Still trying to make me believe you're a tough troublemaker? Sorry. It won't work. Although I will say that you have caused *me* plenty of trouble. And a number of sleepless nights. I hope tonight won't be one of those sleepless nights."

"Maybe you'd sleep better if you had a teddy bear of your own," she commented.

"Care to apply for the job?" he countered.

"No, thanks. I'm already overworked as it is. Managing The Toy Chest and helping Ellie with the toy museum are more than enough to keep me busy."

"How do you plan on acquiring enough toys to start the museum?"

At one time, she realized, she would have answered his question with a flip remark about stealing them, but because he was asking seriously, she answered him seriously. "We hope to start out with loans, not of money, but of toys. Ellie has a sizable collection of her own, which will be the basis for the museum's collection. I've got a few things I've picked up over the years, and we've got two other collectors in the area who have agreed to put their collections on long-term loan to the museum. With this base we plan on filling in what bare spots there might be with a few additional purchases and a lot of publicity so that others will want to donate or lend some of their toys." She paused.

"Why are you looking at me that way? Are you surprised that I actually know what I'm talking about? I have put a lot of thought and research into this project, you know."

"If I was looking at you differently, it was in appreciation. Your normal reaction when I've asked about the museum has been to answer me with defensive quips. I'm glad to see that you finally trust me enough to talk to me."

Lisa didn't know what to say to that. Did she trust Bryce? Was that why she'd spoken to him more openly than she had before? But trust was a two-way street, and it was a street both of them were just beginning to traverse. Where would it end up taking them? She didn't know. The only thing she was really certain of was that they were almost in Nevada City.

Their first stop was the American Victorian museum. The museum was housed in the old Miner's Foundry and dated back to 1856. The red frame building was also the home of a local radio station. Lisa waved at the disc jockey as she walked by the broadcasting booth.

"You know that guy?" Bryce asked with what sounded suspiciously like jealousy.

Lisa nodded. "I've been here for the teddy bear convention they put on each year. I met him then."

"If you've already been here before, why come again?"

"Because I wasn't visiting it then with the intention of being involved with a museum of our own. Now I want to have another look and take notes on the displays. This museum plays a large role in the city. They have concerts and plays here."

"And teddy bear conventions, apparently."

"That's right."

"Do you have any idea where you'll be housing Ellie's toy museum?"

"We haven't decided yet. She mentioned the house as being one temporary setting."

"Her house?"

"Yes." Lisa turned to look at him. "Something wrong with that?"

"Where will Ellie live when her house is turned into a museum?"

"I didn't say the house *was* going to become a museum, just that it was an option as a temporary site. And during that time Ellie would still live in the house, probably on the second floor, while the first floor would become the museum. You said yourself that it was a large place and had plenty of extra room."

As they walked around the museum, Lisa took notes and made sketches while Bryce was preoccupied with his own thoughts. The fact that Ellie was willing to give up her own house, even if it was only the first floor and even if it was only temporarily, made him realize how committed she was to this toy museum idea of hers. And he had to admit, it sounded as if his grandmother and Lisa had put a great deal of thought into the project. It wasn't the spur-of-the-moment idea that he'd first suspected.

Lisa noticed Bryce's silence and wondered what he was thinking about. He looked serious. He also looked good. He was actually wearing a pair of jeans, the first time she'd seen him wearing casual clothes. His polo shirt was blue once again. He seemed to favor that color, and she had to admit that it did nice things to his eyes. His eyes, however, were now doing naughty things to her.

It was hard for her to pretend not to notice when he was gazing at her so intently. Lisa didn't think there was *that* much to see. She was dressed as casually as he was. She, too, wore jeans, although hers had seen more wear than his. The red short-sleeved shirt she wore was covered by a denim jacket. Her red bandanna, tied around her throat, added a saucy touch that she liked. Apparently he did, too.

Their eyes met.

Bryce cleared his throat. "Are you just about done here?"

She nodded.

"Lunch?" He grabbed on to the word as if seeking a safe mooring in choppy waters. "Do you have any preferences?"

Lots of them, but none of them has anything to do with lunch! Come on, Lisa, she told herself. *Think. Try to sound coherent.* "I'm really not all that familiar with the restaurants here. Let's just walk around and stop when some place catches our fancy. Walking is the best way to see the town, anyway."

"Fine." Bryce took hold of her hand as they strolled down Broad Street.

Gaslights lined the main street, preserving the atmosphere of the golden past. But at the moment Lisa was more concerned with preserving her own emotional equilibrium. The loose clasp of his hand made her feel protected and cared for, and that surprised her. She was just getting used to the jolts of awareness and desire she got whenever he touched her, and now she had something new to contend with. Something that was warm and mellow, something she was afraid she might end up wanting too much.

To cover her confusion she jumped into an informative lecture about Nevada City's history, but Bryce gently interrupted her. "You don't have to play the tour guide with me. I'm not here to see the sights. I'm here to be with you."

"Talk like that makes me nervous," she confessed in a voice that was half teasing and half serious.

"Why? Because it's easier to discuss the history of the area than to discuss what's happening between us?"

"Yes."

"Still trying to be prudent?" he asked her softly.

Lisa nodded. Although I'm not sure I'm doing a very good job at it, she thought wistfully.

"It's a losing battle, you know."

"Losing one battle doesn't mean I've lost the war," she retorted.

"Is that how you'd describe what's between us?"

"I don't know how to describe what's between us. You're the one who's got a way with words, not me."

"Oh, I wouldn't say that. You've been able to hold your own in all our verbal confrontations."

"And we've certainly had our fair share of those, haven't we?" she noted ruefully.

"Yes, we have."

"So I guess this means you don't want to hear how the state of Nevada snitched its name from Nevada City, huh?"

"I'd rather hear about you and your feelings for me."

"That isn't the kind of conversation you have in the middle of a crowded sidewalk."

"You're absolutely right. It's the kind of conversation we should have here." He stopped in front of the National Hotel. "This looks like a great place to spend the night. You did say this was an overnight trip, didn't you?"

"That's right, but I've already made arrangements to stay someplace else." And boy, was she grateful that she'd done that. There was something a little too tempting about standing in front of a hotel, talking about spending the night with Bryce. "We're expected."

He did not look pleased. "Expected by whom?"

"I'll tell you over lunch."

He frowned at her. "Then we'd better eat soon. As you may have noticed, patience is not my strong suit when I'm around you."

"I think there's a restaurant around the corner at the top of the hill."

As they approached the corner, they passed a commemorative plaque. Knowing what it said, Lisa smiled as Bryce quickly scanned it.

THE LADIES OF THE EVENING
To commemorate that ubiquitous segment of society
who have been unacknowledged. Who though obscure,
made an essential contribution
to the settlement of the west.

"You know, that's one of the few things you haven't accused me of so far," she murmured in amusement. "Being a lady of the evening."

Her words conjured up such a provocative picture in his mind that Bryce was momentarily speechless. The sudden fantasy was very vivid, very intense, just like his feelings for Lisa.

Seeing his glassy eyes, she said, "Hey, I was just kidding. We'd better get you to a restaurant—you're looking a little pale."

"It's nothing. I'm merely trying to restrain myself from ravishing you right here and now. Nothing to be concerned about." He gave her the wolfish smile of a gambler. "But I bet you don't make it to the top of this hill without my kissing you."

She looked at him uncertainly. Bryce didn't seem the type for this sort of shenanigans, especially in broad daylight. "Are you serious?"

"Definitely. I'll even give you a head start." He released her hand.

"You're on." She was off in a flash.

Even so, it wasn't much of a race, because he never gave her the head start he'd promised her. He caught her before she'd gone more than a few yards. Putting his arms around her waist, he lifted her until the soles of her scuffed western boots were several inches off the ground.

Lisa braced her hands on his shoulders as she laughingly looked down at his face. "You cheated!"

"Damn right," he agreed.

"Now what?"

"Now you kiss me."

"Right here?" She looked around at the other people passing them by.

He nodded, slowly sliding her down his body until her feet were back on the ground. Then he took her hand and brought it up to his lips. "Right here."

Never one to welch on a bet, Lisa did kiss him. It might have been brief, but it was potent and it left them both shaken and inexplicably pleased.

They stood there for a moment, staring into each other's eyes, just smiling until the jostling of the surrounding pedestrian traffic reawakened them to their surroundings.

"Uh, lunch, right?" Lisa said, trying to place their activities before the unexpected bout of fooling around.

"Right." He released her with marked reluctance.

The restaurant on the top of the hill turned out to be an English tearoom that specialized in lunches and high teas.

After they'd gotten their food, Bryce looked at her choice and shook his head. "Only in California would you find someone eating authentic English steak and kidney pie with a glass of grapefruit juice."

"Variety is the spice of life," she retorted.

Bryce suddenly realized that Lisa was the spice of his life. She made him happy. She made him feel like a kid again while also making him feel like more of a man than he'd ever felt with any other woman. She was fiercely loyal and protective of those she loved. What would it be like to be loved by her? Heaven, sheer heaven. And he planned on experiencing it very soon.

"So tell me, what are these plans you've got for tonight?" he asked her. "Who's expecting us?"

"My parents."

He was surprised by the news. "They're expecting you to stop by for a visit?"

"Of sorts, yes."

"I thought they were out prospecting in the countryside someplace."

"They are."

"You're planning on going out into the countryside to see them?"

"No. We arranged to meet at a friend's house."

"How far is it from here?"

"About an hour's drive. Why?" she asked him.

"We could always come back here and stay at the hotel."

"No, you don't understand. We'll be staying the night with my parents at their friends' house."

"That might have been the plan before I came along, but I'm sure they wouldn't want to put up a stranger."

"These friends of my parents, the Bakers, are renovating a large Victorian house. They plan on turning it into a bed-and-breakfast, so there are plenty of rooms available."

His eyes narrowed. "You knew all this ahead of time, didn't you? That's why you didn't protest when I said I was coming along. Because you knew we'd be chaperoned tonight by your parents."

"You're the one who insisted on coming along," she reminded him. "I didn't make these plans for you or because of you. They were made before you threatened to follow me.

Besides, you've been asking me so many questions about my parents that I thought you'd like to meet them."

"What have you told them about me?"

"Nothing. I thought you'd want to fill them in yourself."

"Thanks a lot."

"You're welcome. We'd better get going. We don't want to be late." She picked up the check. When it looked as if he was about to argue, she said, "You paid for dinner last night. Now it's my turn."

"Keeping track, are you?"

"I don't like to feel—"

"Beholden to anyone. Yes, I know. I remember you telling me that. But you never did tell me *why* you feel that way."

"It's just the way I am."

"Like the color of your hair or your eyes, right?"

"Something like that," she said.

"I don't buy that."

"You don't have to. I'm buying, remember?"

"And you remember this, I can be very persistent. Each time you avoid a question, I become even more determined to know the answer."

"A character flaw of yours, I know."

He ignored her comment. "So just because I'm letting you off easy this time, don't think you can get away with it forever."

Forever wasn't a word that applied to the two of them, Lisa thought. Bryce would be returning to Chicago in another week. He'd forget all about her. She hoped to be able to do the same about him, but she was beginning to have her doubts. Bryce wasn't a man one would forget very easily.

"What are your parents going to think when they see you've brought a man along with you?" he asked as they neared the small town where the rendezvous had been arranged.

"What's the matter? Getting cold feet?" Teasing him helped alleviate her own nervousness. "Afraid they're going to wrangle you into a shotgun wedding?"

Bryce was not amused. "Has it occurred to you that I might just be nervous about meeting your parents because they *are* your parents, and for no other reason?"

"Listen, after coping with the family you've got, I think mine is a piece of cake. They're nice people, like Ellie."

In the end Bryce's tenseness ended up rubbing off on her, so that by the time they arrived *he* was calm and *she* was the jumpy one.

"Maybe this wasn't such a good idea after all," she muttered. "There's a motel a couple miles down the road. You might be more comfortable there."

"Now who's getting cold feet?" He took her hand and led her up the front steps. "Come on. How bad can it be?"

The door was suddenly opened by a bear of a man who looked at them and then yelled over his shoulder, "Better get out the shotgun, Tom. Your little girl's brought company!"

Six

_____

He's only kidding," Lisa hastily reassured an uncertain-looking Bryce. "Max Baker and my father have known each other a long time. They're both a pair of practical jokers."

"Now, is that any way to talk to your elders?" Max demanded, having heard the tail end of her explanation. "Come on in here and give me a hug." As Lisa obliged, he engulfed her in a bear hug before exclaiming, "I swear, girl, you get taller each time I see you. You still growin' or what?"

"And don't let his quaint accent fool you," Lisa added for Bryce's benefit. "Max here is from Boston."

"Blasphemy, girl! Why, my family's been in these parts for donkey's years."

"Translated that means he's been here two years," Lisa said, then went on to make the introductions. "This is Bryce's first trip to this area. I'm showing him some of the sights. I knew you and Iris wouldn't mind if I brought him along. Consider him your first out-of-state guest.''

"Welcome to The Mother Lode Inn,'' Max said as he shook Bryce's hand. "We're not officially open yet, but we're pleased to have you stay. Where are you from?''

"Chicago,'' Bryce replied, somewhat absently, for his attention had turned to the tall man who'd just joined them. Was this Lisa's father? His appearance surprised Bryce. He looked more like an absent-minded professor than a gold prospector.

"Daddy!'' Lisa went from Max's arms to her father's. She hugged him tightly. He'd always been Daddy to her, and he always would be. He'd never quite grown up to be a *Dad*, and *Father* didn't suit him—it was too formal.

"Hi, honey.'' He kissed her cheek. "What was Max bellowing about you having brought company?''

"Daddy, I'd like you to meet Bryce Stephenson, Ellie's grandson. Bryce, this is my father, Tom Cantrell.''

The two men sized each other up as they shook hands.

"Your grandmother is a fine woman,'' Tom said.

"Thank you, sir.''

"Call me Tom. 'Sir' makes me feel old.''

Bryce smiled. "Tom it is, then.''

"Well, come on in,'' Max invited, "and meet our better halves.''

Bryce had no trouble telling which of the two women in the Victorian parlor was Lisa's mother. Although not quite as tall as Lisa, she had the same blue-gray eyes.

Lisa's words confirmed it. "That lovely lady over there on the couch is Max's wife, Iris.'' Iris waved at him. "And this lovely lady is my mother, Anita Cantrell. Mom, this is Bryce Stephenson, Ellie's grandson.''

"And a friend of your daughter's,'' Bryce added, having gotten fed up with being referred to exclusively as Ellie's grandson. "I'm very glad to meet you, Mrs. Cantrell. I've heard a lot about you from your daughter."

"You have?" Anita looked from Bryce to Lisa and back again.

Bryce nodded and casually dropped an arm around Lisa's shoulders.

"Ignore him," Lisa advised her mother. "Bryce is a terrible tease, just like Daddy."

"Hey, I've been called many things in my life, but never a *terrible* tease," Bryce retorted with one of his devastating smiles.

"There's a first time for everything," she shot back, stepping out of his reach.

"So tell me about yourself, Bryce," Anita suggested.

"It's either that or you can come and help Tom and me grill the hamburgers out back," Max interjected, taking pity on him.

Anita frowned. "Since when does it take three grown men to grill a few hamburger patties?"

"Since the beginning of time." Tom and Max smiled conspiratorially.

"We'll talk later, Mrs. Cantrell," Bryce promised.

"Smooth, isn't he?" her mother noted after the men had gone outside.

Lisa nodded. "Too smooth, sometimes. I'm trying to cure him of that."

"Really? This sounds serious."

"It's not. I told you, he's Ellie's grandson."

"And he said he was a friend of yours."

"He was exaggerating."

"How long have you known him?"

"About a week."

"I think there are sparks here," Anita stated. "What do you think, Iris?"

"I agree." Iris nodded. "Unmistakable sparks. Did you see the way he looked at her? And the way she looked at him? Better than on the soaps."

Lisa shifted restlessly. "Would you two give me a break?"

"Bringing a good-looking man like that to meet your parents is bound to give them ideas," Iris explained. "I'll leave you two alone to work it out while I go make the salad." With a cheerful wave, she left the room.

Anita turned to her daughter once again. "So tell me, what's with you and Bryce?"

"Nothing."

"I'm your mother. You can't fool me. Something's going on here."

After ten more minutes of questioning, Lisa began wondering if bringing Bryce along had been such a good idea after all. She hadn't anticipated that her mother would be so curious. She was grateful when her father's return brought her mother's inquisition to a temporary halt.

However, her father had a few questions of his own. "Your Mr. Stephenson keeps giving me strange looks. How come?" Tom asked.

"First off, he's not *my* Mr. Stephenson. He's just Ellie's grandson, that's all."

"I thought Ellie didn't get along with her family," Tom said.

"She doesn't with most of them, but she's got a soft spot for Bryce."

"How about you? Do you have a soft spot for Bryce, too?" Anita asked.

"No way!"

"Then why did you bring him along with you?" her father asked.

"He insisted."

"Really? Why would he do that?"

Lisa was tempted to tell her parents the whole story but realized that it might make the evening awkward. She didn't think her parents would find anything humorous in Bryce's initial assumption that she was after Ellie's money. And for some reason she didn't want them and Bryce to get off on the wrong foot. So she kept quiet about their earlier misunderstandings and only told her parents part of the truth.

"Bryce wanted to see Nevada City. It's his first visit to this area."

"What have you told him about us?" her father asked. "Does he know that we're prospecting for gold? Is that why he looked at us so strangely when he first came in?"

"He knows you're prospecting, but he probably looked at you strangely because of what Max said about getting out your shotgun. After hearing that, Bryce was no doubt expecting you to look more like a prospector—a bearded stranger who carries everything he owns on the back of a mule."

Lisa's description made Tom smile. "Well, I did try that beard last year, but your mother complained about it itching her, so I had to shave it off."

"And you know what a softy your father is where animals are concerned," her mother added. "He'd rather carry the load himself than make a poor mule carry it."

"I just have the four-wheel drive Jeep carry it and then we're all happy," Tom said.

"Except for your young man." Anita pointed out the window to where Bryce was helping Max with the grill. "He still looks a little dazed."

"He's not *my* young man, Mom!" Lisa's voice was filled with exasperation. "I already told you that. And if he looks dazed, it's probably because he hasn't had much experience grilling hamburgers."

"He's not rich, is he?" Tom asked.

Lisa nodded. "I'm afraid he is."

"Oh, honey..."

"I know, I know. Now do you believe me when I say that he's just Ellie's grandson and nothing more? You two, of all people, should know how I feel about the subject of crown princes of wealthy families."

Her parents didn't push her any further.

They all sat down to dinner a short while later. The menu was plain—hamburgers, baked potatoes and a tossed salad, with chilled bottles of beer to wash it all down.

Bryce drank his beer from the bottle, the same way her father and Max did. The problem was that Lisa couldn't seem to keep her eyes away from Bryce for longer than a second or two. She noticed that he had a slight cleft in his chin. How could she have missed that? You are definitely going off the deep end, she chastised herself. Eat your hamburger and stop eyeing Bryce as if he were on the menu.

Luckily her father and Max were so busy telling tall tales of the gold rush era that her silence wasn't noticeable.

"But the best story of all is the story of Black Bart," Tom stated dramatically.

Knowing a cue when he heard one, Bryce asked, "Who's Black Bart?"

Tom, a natural storyteller, waggled his eyebrows in disbelief of anyone not having heard of Black Bart. "Why, he was the finest road agent ever."

"Road agent?" Bryce repeated.

Lisa translated for him. "Road agent—thief. Bandit. Highway robber."

"He pulled off thirty robberies without ever firing a shot." Tom shook his head in admiration. "They called him the Gentleman Bandit. Always said please, never swore, never drank liquor..."

"And was a very natty dresser," Lisa interjected.

"Who's telling this story?" her father demanded.

"Sorry," Lisa said with a meekness that made Bryce grin.

"Now, where was I?" Tom paused to rub his chin. "Oh, yes. Now, the way I heard the story, Bart's real name was Charles Boles, and he started out as a high-class, educated man who taught school in the northern mines. But he loved a practical joke. One day he was riding along the road after school, when he heard the stage coming. Since he knew the stagecoach driver, he thought he'd play a trick on him. So he hid his horse in the bushes, tied a handkerchief over his face and broke a branch off a bush—a branch that was just about the size and shape of a pistol. When the stage came along, he stepped out onto the road and told the driver to halt. The stage stopped. Since there was no one riding shotgun, he continued with the charade, telling the driver to throw down the Wells Fargo box from under the seat. The driver did, and the box landed on the ground with such a force that Charles Boles, alias Black Bart, jumped back in surprise. The driver, thinking this was his chance, whipped the horses into a gallop and the stage took off again, leaving Boles and the treasure behind. The box was filled with gold bullion bars and coins and sacks of gold dust. Looking at the riches surrounding him, Boles decided to quit teaching and stick to practical joking."

"Was he ever caught?" Bryce questioned.

That was the lawyer in him asking, Lisa thought. Aloud she said, "Just wait and see."

"Well, Bart continued prospecting for gold in Wells Fargo's boxes. He always laid careful plans, worked alone and never struck near home. He'd taken the money from his first haul and banked it down in San Francisco. He set up residence in a nice hotel and told them he was a mining man who'd be going out of town from time to time. By now Black Bart was carrying a real gun, a double-barreled shotgun, but he never used it and he never robbed a passenger. But when he robbed the Wells Fargo boxes, he'd leave behind a note signed Black Bart with the letters *P* and *o* and the figure *8*. Get it?''

Bryce shook his head.

"Po8 was his pun for poet.'' Tom chuckled. "Now, there's no telling how long Black Bart could have kept going if he hadn't been such a natty dresser, as my daughter put it. When he was slightly injured in a robbery over near Copperopolis, they found one of his shirt cuffs, which had a laundry mark on it. None of the laundries around here used such a marking, so they took it down into San Francisco and checked the laundries there. It took them a while, but they finally located the laundry and then Black Bart. They brought him in, and he finally confessed to the last robbery, but none of the others. He was found guilty and sentenced to six years in San Quentin.''

"Ah...'' Bryce nodded. "So justice was finally done.''

Tom held up his hand. "But wait, there's more. Legend has it that a spate of robberies started up again right after Black Bart's release from prison. He was so well disguised that no one could ever identify him, but the Wells Fargo detectives recognized the style of the robberies. When they finally located Black Bart, they offered him a deal. He was getting pretty old by then. So Wells Fargo ended up giving him a pension with the stipulation that he wouldn't rob them anymore.''

"That's it? That's the end of the story?''

"Of course,'' Tom said, as if any fool would know the story had ended.

"Oh.'' As Bryce looked around the table he could almost read their minds. *No sense of humor,* they were probably thinking. *Bad sign.* "Uh, great story,'' he said with an awkwardness that was foreign to him. Normally he was able to get along very well with people—after all, a great deal of his work depended on his smoothing the way between clients with differing views. But now that he was in a personal rather than a professional situation, he felt somewhat out of his element. He felt even more so after hearing Lisa's father's next comment.

"So tell me, Bryce, what are your intentions toward my daughter?"

Lisa almost choked. "Daddy, stop teasing! He's only kidding," she hastily reassured Bryce.

Bryce answered the question anyway. "My intention is to figure out what makes your daughter tick."

Tom chuckled and shook his head. "I don't know. You've set a tough task for yourself, son. She's my daughter. I've known her all her life, and *I* still haven't completely figured her out. That's part of a woman's charm, you know. Her mother's the same way. They're the kind of women that grab hold of your heart and don't let go."

"Now, that's enough teasing," Anita declared with a blush. "Bryce, you were going to tell me about yourself earlier, before we got into all this talk about local folklore. It's an unusual name, Bryce. Is it a family name?"

"No. I'm told that I was given the name because I was born nine months after my parents took a trip to Bryce Canyon in Utah."

"Good thing they didn't take a trip to Schenectady," Tom said.

"You've got a point," Bryce agreed. "Lisa tells me you're doing some gold prospecting."

"That's right."

"It's an unusual occupation."

"Oh, it's not an occupation. It's for fun."

"Fun?" Bryce repeated as if he'd never heard of the word.

"Fun. Naturally we hope to find gold, but we're sure having fun looking."

"How long have you been looking?"

"Oh, off and on for—what?" Tom paused to look at Anita for confirmation. "Almost ten years now, I guess. Of course, the only time we can really do much prospecting is in the spring and early summer. There's too much snow in winter, and by fall a lot of the creek beds have dried up."

"What do you do when you're not prospecting?"

"Something different each year. Sometimes we head down to Arizona. One year we drove clear over to Florida to visit Disney World. You remember that, Anita? We got stuck in that huge snow storm in Utah and spent two days at a truck stop. We made a lot of new friends that year."

Wondering where they'd gotten the money for all this traveling, Bryce said, "You two seem to get around a lot."

"We sure do," Tom agreed.

Lisa recognized that speculative gleam in Bryce's eye. "Bryce has an insatiable curiosity about people. Comes from his being a lawyer, I guess." Actually she was afraid it came from his being suspicious. She gave him a look that made it clear she wouldn't allow him to interrogate her parents.

"Ah, well, loose lips sink ships," her father told Bryce.

Bryce frowned in confusion. "I beg your pardon?"

"Something I learned from an old prospector. Around here people are pretty close-mouthed about their claims. We don't talk much about the details of our activities. A few of our neighbors along the river are quite paranoid about it. They don't like strangers nosing around at all. They've even got signs posted saying Beware of Buckshot If Claim Jumping. Not that we've had much trouble so far, but with the fluctuating price of gold, it's a safety measure. Nothing personal, you understand. It's just that we have to be careful."

"Naturally." Bryce's voice was carefully neutral.

Lisa sighed. She could imagine what Bryce was thinking now—picturing her father aiming a shotgun at intruders. Quite a different picture from his own family, she was sure. How often did the Stephensons get together and grill hamburgers and eat sooty baked potatoes? As for having to beware of buckshot...

Lisa could tell by the look on Bryce's face that he was attempting to figure her parents out. "Stop trying," she softly advised him as the others began talking about something else.

He turned to look at her. "What?"

"You've got your hands full trying to figure *me* out. Don't add my parents to the project. We're just not the type to fit into neat little prelabeled boxes. We're a vanishing breed called individuals."

"Ah, an endangered species."

She grinned. "So I've been told."

"You two want some of the brownies, or do we get to eat them all ourselves?" Tom asked them.

"If those brownies are from my favorite bakery in Grass Valley, I want the whole bag myself," Lisa retorted.

"I swear, these brownies and Columbia are your two main weak spots," her mother retorted.

"What's Columbia?" Bryce asked, immediately interested in Lisa's weak spots.

"A restored ghost town that's been turned into a state park," Tom replied. "It's not far from Jamestown. I'm surprised Lisa hasn't taken you there yet." In an aside to Lisa, Tom added, "You'll have to show him."

Personally, Bryce planned on having Lisa show him a lot more than some restored ghost town. But for the time being he'd have to settle for what he could get.

What he ended up getting was a guest bedroom across the hall from Lisa's. Just knowing that she was so close by made it impossible for him to get any sleep.

Lisa was suffering from a similar problem herself. She tried counting sheep, but they all ended up looking like wolves with Bryce's blue eyes and irresistible smile. Feeling decidedly edgy, she tossed off the covers and jumped out of bed. She needed something to relax her, a glass of warm milk, maybe. With that in mind, she slipped a silk kimono over her nightgown and reached for the bedroom door-knob. Pausing a moment, she listened to make sure that no one else was up and about, but all was quiet.

Lisa opened the door to her room just as Bryce was opening the door to his room.

He saw her.

She saw him.

They both froze.

Lisa couldn't take her eyes off him. This was a Bryce she hadn't seen before. His chest was bare, and his jeans rode low on his hips. His blond hair was sexily rumpled, as if he'd run impatient fingers through it. Only the hunger in his eyes was familiar.

Bryce couldn't believe his eyes. Lisa was standing in the soft glow of the light from her room, a position that made her thin robe practically invisible. The nightgown she wore beneath the robe was also backlit, allowing him to see the outline of her long legs. He couldn't breathe, and he didn't move, almost fearing she might be a vision of his imagination and not reality.

He looked into her eyes, and what he saw there made him take a step forward.

Then the spell was abruptly shattered by the sound of someone loudly climbing the stairs. Anita's and Tom's voices were clearly audible as they reached the landing. With a regretful look on her part, and a fiercely frustrated one on his, Lisa and Bryce stepped back into their individual rooms and shut the door on their shared fantasy.

Not tonight maybe, but soon, Bryce vowed. Because he couldn't take much more of this.

Seven

The last thing Bryce needed when he returned to Ellie's house the next day was a lecture. But that's exactly what he got. Ellie was waiting for him the minute he walked in the front door. She had her hands on her hips, a sure sign that she was upset. "All right, Bryce. What are you up to? And I want the truth."

"The truth is that I don't know what you're talking about."

"I'm talking about the fact that you and Lisa were gone all night. You just took off, no warning, leaving me a note saying you'd gone to Nevada City and would be back today."

"And I did come back today. We both did." In fact, Bryce had dropped Lisa off at The Toy Chest before coming to his grandmother's house.

"You've been spending an awful lot of time with Lisa and I'd like to know why."

Bryce tried not to smile as she fixed him with a relentless stare that reminded him of a nurse dealing with a recalcitrant patient. Even though she was a good six inches shorter than he was, Ellie still managed to look intimidating. His grandmother wanted some straight answers, and she clearly wasn't going to leave him alone until he gave them to her. "Lisa is an exciting woman. I'd like to get to know her better."

"Does this interest of yours have something to do with your disapproval of the toy museum? Are you trying to charm Lisa so you can convince her to leave me and all my Stephenson money alone?"

"You and Lisa really do think an awful lot alike, do you know that? She's already accused me of the same thing herself."

"And?" Ellie prompted him.

"And I'll tell you the same thing I told her. That having spent all that time with her, I no longer believe she would do anything to hurt you. She cares a great deal about you. She's also very protective of you. And it's clear that you're equally protective of her. But you don't have to protect her from me. I won't hurt her."

To his surprise, Ellie looked even more concerned than she had before.

"Are you beginning to have feelings for her, Bryce? Because if you are, you'd better stop."

"Why do you say that?"

"Because no good can come of it."

"I thought grandmothers were supposed to enjoy matchmaking," he noted irritably. "Why are you so set against the idea of Lisa and me getting together?"

"Lisa's already been hurt. I don't want to see you or your family hurt her any further. But Lisa's not the only one I worry about. I'm worried about you, too. Your family would never approve of Lisa. Surely you know that. And if your feelings for her are real, and were to progress into something serious, then the situation is bound to get very sticky, indeed."

"I think you're exaggerating."

"I'm thinking ahead, Bryce, and I see nothing but trouble for the two of you."

He gave her a reassuring pat on the shoulder. "You worry too much."

"A bad trait I seem to have picked up from you," she retorted.

"Well, if it will set your mind at ease, Lisa and I did not spend the night *alone* together. We stopped at a friend's inn and spent the night there along with her parents. Needless to say, Lisa and I had separate rooms."

"Lisa had you meet her parents?"

Bryce nodded.

"What did you think of them?"

"They . . . different."

"They may seem different to you, but not to Lisa. She's very close to her parents."

"I know she is. And I didn't mean it as a criticism of them. But I find it a little hard to understand how they can live with so little planning and forethought."

"They have a dream."

"I know. They actually told me they're prospecting because it's fun."

"A foreign notion to you, I'm sure," Ellie remarked dryly.

Bryce nodded. "You play a game of racquetball because it's fun. You don't take up gold prospecting."

"You see? This is what I'm talking about. You and Lisa are just too different."

"Which is why I'm trying to see things from her perspective. Lisa's taking me over to Columbia tomorrow. Maybe then I can get a better idea of this fascination her family has with gold prospecting."

"You don't have to wait until tomorrow. I can take you to Columbia this afternoon," Ellie said. "But you'd rather have Lisa take you, right? Because you want to see *her*, not Columbia. I could make sure she has to work tomorrow, you know. She *does* manage my toy store, after all."

"You could do that, but you won't."

"What makes you think I won't?"

"Because you care about Lisa. And so do I. So stop worrying. Everything's going to be fine. You'll see."

"I wish I could be sure of that," Ellie muttered as Bryce left to go check in with the office in Chicago.

Lisa and Bryce's visit to Columbia got off to an exciting start as Lisa yelled, "Watch out for the stagecoach!" When Bryce didn't immediately heed her warning, she grabbed his arm and pulled him out of the way. "Why didn't you move?" she demanded.

"I thought you were kidding."

He watched the full-size stagecoach as it rumbled up the hill and proceeded to the Wells Fargo station in town.

"This is Columbia," she reminded him. "Cars aren't allowed on the main street, but stagecoaches are, so watch out for them, okay?"

"They really take this historic thing seriously here, don't they?"

"You bet. Columbia is the only officially preserved gold town in the United States. You should see the place in summer. It's really hopping then. They even have a tent city behind town with actors all dressed in period costume. But at least they've got the stagecoach running now. Want to ride on it?'' she asked him.

"No, thanks."

She was disappointed. She *always* rode the stagecoach when she came to Columbia. "Why not?"

Bryce had no intention of admitting that he got motion sickness when he was in small, enclosed places. Instead, he said, "Why would anyone want to ride on a bumpy stagecoach?"

"For the magic. For the fun of it. Do you ever do anything just for fun?"

"I play racquetball."

"Big deal. I mean something meaningful."

"Riding on a stagecoach is meaningful?"

It is to me, she thought to herself, but suddenly felt awkward admitting it out loud. Bryce was making her feel foolish, which in turn made her defensive. "I suppose you were too busy reading law books to ever play cowboys and Indians as a kid. This all seems pretty silly to you, doesn't it? You didn't really want to see Columbia at all. You could care less about the magic of the wild West. All you see here are bricks and mortar."

"I also see a woman who looks beautiful when she's angry." Observing the way her expression darkened, he held out his hands in a placating way. "Okay, okay, I was only kidding. If you must know the truth—yes, I did play cowboys and Indians as a kid. There, are you happy now?"

"Not yet, but I suppose it's a start. Just let yourself feel. Close your eyes and imagine what it must have been like."

But when Bryce closed his eyes, all he could think of was Lisa—the sweet smell of her, the warmth of her body pressed against his. He sighed. He was imagining, all right, but not about the gold rush.

"Can you see it?" she asked.

"I can see it, all right." The two of them, naked, stretched out on a bed, making love. The image was so strong it was all he could do not to reach out and pull her into his arms.

"You know, a lot of movies are filmed here," she was saying.

He wished he could film his fantasy of her. Regretfully, he opened his eyes.

The hungry way he was eyeing her made Lisa feel decidedly nervous. She struggled to maintain her train of thought. "Umm, movies. Yes, umm, they film a lot of movies here."

"You already said that." Bryce moved closer. "You seem a little distracted. Something bothering you?"

"*You're* bothering me, and you know it. You're doing it on purpose."

"Guilty as charged. You see, Lisa, I don't intend to let you forget what we have between us."

"What do you want from me?"

"I want you. And I think you want me, too."

"I'll get over it," she retorted wryly.

"No, you won't. I'll make sure of it."

"Pretty confident, aren't you?"

"I have to be around you. You haven't exactly done much to build up my ego."

"Your ego is already too inflated. Probably the result of your having been fawned over by too many women."

"Where did you get an idea like that?" Seeing her guilty expression, he said, "No, let me guess. You've been talking to Ellie about me."

Not wanting to cause any friction between Bryce and Ellie, Lisa quickly clarified things. "She didn't go into any details. She just happened to mention that a lot of women find you attractive."

"And did Ellie warn you away from her grandson the lady killer?"

"Of course not. Ellie knows I can take care of myself."

"Ellie worries about you the same way you worry about her."

Something in his voice made her add, "She worries about you, too, Bryce. Ellie loves you."

"Even if she doesn't quite trust me."

"You just have different priorities, that's all. You're a bottom-line kind of guy. That's fine, but you have to accept that other people have different priorities from yours."

"And what are your priorities?" he asked her.

"Enjoying life, enjoying the people I love. What about you?"

"Before meeting you, I probably would have said my main priority was to succeed. Now I'm not so sure. You've made me realize there's more to life. I don't know what to call it yet, but I do know there's something more."

"That's an encouraging sign. There may be hope for you yet, Bryce."

"I'm glad you've finally realized that."

They looked at each other. For Lisa, time suddenly lost its perspective there in the brilliant sunshine.

"We will be together, Lisa," he murmured seductively. "Soon, very soon."

She shook her head, slowly at first and then more emphatically. "We've only known each other for nine days," she reminded him. "You'll be going back to Chicago in another week."

"Would you miss me if I go?"

"What do you mean *if* you go?"

"Would you miss me?" he repeated.

She paused, then admitted, "Yes, but I'll get over that, too."

"You'll get over wanting me, missing me? Seems to me like a lot of wasted energy. I can think of better ways to use that energy."

"I'm sure you can." She gave him an exasperated look. "Why is it that you always seem to hold these very personal conversations in the middle of the street?"

"Because I haven't been able to get you someplace more intimate, like a hotel, yet. But I haven't given up trying."

"So I've noticed."

"Then perhaps you've also noticed how gentlemanly and patient I've been so far."

"Actually, I hadn't noticed that, no."

"In that case—" he snared her in his arms "—maybe I should just kiss you right here."

"You seem to be making a habit out of accosting me on street corners," she noted with a grin. It was difficult...no, make that downright impossible to resist him when he was in this kind of teasing mood.

"It's one of the few places where I can get you alone."

"I hate to break this to you, Bryce, but we are not alone."

"Feels like we are."

Lisa felt the same way. Her excitement grew as Bryce startled her by stealing a quick kiss before letting her go.

"Okay," he said. "Now you can show me Columbia."

"In five seconds or less, right?"

"Listen, I like western towns as much as the next guy."

"Sure you do," she said with teasing disbelief.

"Are you deliberately tempting me to kiss you again?"

"Hey, if there's any tempting being done, you're the one who's doing it."

"Getting to you, am I?"

"You know you are. Tell me something—is this the way you usually conduct your romantic pursuits?"

"You make it sound as if I do nothing all day long but chase women. If that was the case, I'd hardly have time to spend on my law practice, and I can tell you that the practice does take an incredible amount of my time. This is the first vacation I've had for the past three years."

"But it's not a real vacation, is it?" she countered quietly. "You're still working, taking care of family business."

"I've told you before and I'll say it again. I am *not* spending time with you because of your relationship with my grandmother. I'm more interested in establishing a relationship with you myself."

"Why?"

"Because you shake me up. I've never met anyone like you."

"Is that good or bad?"

"Good, I think, but I've stopped trying to figure it out."

"Does that mean you've stopped trying to figure *me* out?" she asked.

"No, it means I'm trying to take things one day at a time, one step at a time. But it's not easy, because every time I look at you I want to make love to you."

"It's not easy for me, either," she whispered.

"Stagecoach! Coming through!" It took the shouted warning to bring them back to the reality surrounding them. This time Bryce grabbed Lisa's arm and pulled her out of the way.

"Let's stay on the sidewalks," he suggested wryly. "Maybe we'll be safer that way."

Lisa knew her security would continue to be in jeopardy simply by her being with Bryce. Each time he looked at her, she found it harder to look away. Each time he touched her, a little more of her resistance melted, and it was now reaching dangerously low proportions. She sighed.

"What was that for?" he asked.

"Nothing."

They moved on, strolling down the wooden sidewalk. They'd been walking about a block when Lisa suddenly detected the wonderful aroma of freshly made fudge.

"Come on." She quickened her step. "There's a wonderful candy store just down here, and unless my nose is mistaken, they've just whipped up a batch of chocolate peanut butter fudge."

Bryce didn't think there was anything mistaken about her nose. He liked the way it sort of tilted up at the end. But then he liked a lot of things about Lisa. The way she filled out a pair of jeans, the way she filled out the T-shirt she was wearing. Then there were the subtle things—the ones he was discovering every moment he spent with her. Like the way she'd tilt her head and give him a sideways look with a matching mischievous smile. Like the way she walked—with the determination of someone who knew where she was going and couldn't wait to get there.

There in this case turned out to be a building with high ceilings and hand-dipped chocolates, as well as the fudge that Lisa had so accurately identified.

Talk about a kid in a candy shop, Bryce thought to himself in amusement. He got a kick out of just watching her. She didn't exactly press that adorable nose of hers against the glass fronting the various displays of candy, but she came real close. By the time they left, Lisa had several little white bags filled with goodies.

"Here, try one." She held out a bag.

"What is it?"

She shook her head. "Boy, talk about being suspicious. It's candy. Do you want to try one or not?"

He reached inside and took one. It looked like a cube of gelatin, coated with powdered sugar, and it didn't taste half-bad. "They're good."

Lisa popped one into her mouth and nodded.

When some of the powdered sugar clung to her moist lips, Bryce couldn't resist reaching out and brushing it away. His index finger gently circled her mouth. Despite the warmth of the day, she shivered.

As she did whenever she was nervous, Lisa launched into speech. "So how do you like Columbia so far?"

"I think I'm hooked," he murmured without taking his eyes, or his caressing finger, away from her lips.

So am I! Lisa thought with whimsical dismay.

Bryce smiled knowingly and brushed his thumb over her lower lip. "Feeling a little warm, are you?"

She responded by playfully nipping his finger with her teeth. "I doubt I'm the only one. I think we could both use some cooling off. How about stopping for a nice cold drink?"

After sipping sarsaparilla in a saloon, they went on to enjoy the sights—stopping to listen to the banjo-playing of a street musician, browsing through a dry goods store filled with everything from bonnets and bola ties to Stetsons and shoes. Bryce was particularly interested in the museum, which displayed mining artifacts and covered the basic evolution of gold prospecting in the area. He hoped to understand more about this fascination Lisa's parents had with gold.

"I guess your parents are doing placer prospecting?" Bryce asked.

She nodded. "You catch on fast."

"Just one of my many talents, ma'am," he drawled.

She already knew about his other talents, charming the socks off her, kissing her senseless, leaving her wanting more and afraid of having it.

They strolled along, hand in hand, enjoying the wonderful spring weather and each other's company, although not necessarily in that order. The tree-shaded streets lined with frame cottages, white picket fences and iron-shuttered brick buildings soon faded into the background as the awareness between them grew. Then they no longer talked, just slowly ambled on, smiling for no reason at all.

"This is your last chance to take a stagecoach ride," she told Bryce once they'd returned to the park's entrance. "They really do a great job with it. They even have a robbery along the route, with a road agent stopping the stage and asking everyone if they've got any gold or silver."

"It sounds like you've done this before."

"Every time I come."

"You can go if you like. I'll wait for you here," Bryce offered.

Lisa shook her head. She didn't want to be apart from Bryce. She could ride the stage anytime. But Bryce was leaving soon, and her time with him was running out.

Lisa managed to block those thoughts from her mind, but she couldn't control her dreams once she'd fallen asleep later that night. They were filled with images of her and Bryce—erotic images, sensual images. A particularly vivid dream of her riding in a stagecoach that had just been held up by Bryce, and his subsequent abduction of her, woke her at four in the morning.

She lay there, breathing quickly. "It was just a dream," she told herself. Rolling over, she sighed and hugged her pillow. "Only a dream," she repeated sleepily. "Too bad."

Bryce was woken up about the same time, but it was the sound of the phone ringing that shattered his dream. He cast a bleary-eyed look at his wristwatch on the bedside table and wondered who could be calling at this hour. Whoever it was, he didn't appreciate the interruption. That dream he'd been having had involved Lisa doing things that made him shiver with pleasure.

With a muttered curse, he hurried out into the hallway and grabbed the phone before it could wake Ellie.

"Hello?" The greeting resembled a growl.

"Bryce, is that you?" Harold demanded.

"Yes, it's me, Uncle." Bryce rubbed a hand over his face, trying to clear his mind. "Is something wrong? Why are you calling in the middle of the night?"

"Middle of the night? It's after six in the morning here. And I'm calling because I just got a call from the private investigator. They came after him with a shotgun! I want to know what's going on out there, Bryce. What kind of people are we dealing with here? They sound desperate to me, and that could be dangerous."

"Wait a minute. Go back to the beginning. Who came after whom with a shotgun?"

"This Cantrell woman's parents came after our investigator, Jones. He was out there checking on them when they fired at him. It's a miracle he wasn't killed!"

"When and where did this incident supposedly happen?"

"There's no supposedly about it. The investigator has no reason to lie about being shot at, Bryce. We don't pay him extra money for battle duty, you know."

"I didn't even know you still had the investigator on this case. Why didn't you tell me?"

"I assumed you realized I'd retain the man's services when he turned up such a thick file on that Cantrell woman."

"She does have a first name," Bryce retorted impatiently. "Her name is Lisa Cantrell."

"Whatever."

"You still didn't answer my original question. Where and when did this happen?"

"I already told you, the incident occurred last night. And it happened out in the middle of no place, where the parents have set up their gold operation."

"That's the answer, then. If Jones was fired upon, it was most likely because he was trespassing on private property. People in gold country are touchy about that sort of thing. They even post notices out here about it. Now that I think about it, Mr. and Mrs. Cantrell did mention that their neighbor was rather paranoid about trespassers."

"When did you meet the parents?"

"A few days ago. Why?"

"Did you get any useful information from them? Did they say anything to incriminate themselves?" Harold answered his own question. "No, I'll bet they're too smart for that."

"Are you listening to me?" Bryce demanded. "I said that the Cantrells probably didn't have anything to do with the shooting. It was most likely their neighbor. They mentioned that he's scared off intruders before. He usually fires warning shots in the air. I'll bet that's what happened. This neighbor saw Jones prowling around and fired a couple of warning shots in the air."

"Are you telling me you believe a cock-and-bull story like that?"

"It's no stranger than the story you concocted about Lisa's parents shooting at Jones and trying to kill him. My interpretation of the facts makes more sense."

"Don't you think it's suspiciously convenient that the parents have a neighbor who shoots at people and that therefore they can blame any incident like this on him? I'm telling you, Bryce, there's more to this case than meets the eye. This isn't just a simple con. I think I may have finally figured out what's going on. I believe this Cantrell woman is syphoning Eleanor's money from the toy museum fund with the intention of using it to further her parents prospecting efforts. Jones did some additional checking on that gold prospecting operation of her parents', and sure enough, a number of small investors have put money into it."

"What's that got to do with anything?"

"Don't you see? It means they need money to keep their search for gold going. And what better way to get money than to take it from a trusting old woman like Eleanor? A little creative bookkeeping and no one would be the wiser."

"Has any money been taken from the toy museum fund?"

"Not yet. It's too soon. They know we're suspicious of them, so they're waiting until our guard is down. That's why I want you to check this out and see what you come up with."

"I've got things here under control," Bryce stated. "But I don't want that investigator stumbling around, creating any more scenes. Take him off the case."

"But—"

Bryce was curt. "You either trust me to take care of things or you don't. Which is it?"

"Of course I trust you."

"Fine. Then tell Jones he's fired. I'll be in touch. Goodbye."

Eight

Bryce tried getting back to sleep after his uncle's call, but it was no use. His mind was awake, even if he wasn't. So he lay in bed, one arm bent under his head, as he stared up at the ceiling and tried to make sense out of this latest development.

The problem was that his uncle's scenario did sound somewhat plausible. If Lisa's parents had investors helping them support their gold prospecting operation, then it was possible that they might need additional assistance, additional funds. But the plan had one major flaw—Lisa would not take money from Ellie, even if it was for her parents. If they needed money, she would be up front about it and ask for a loan.

Which left him where? Still believing in Lisa, but having doubts about her parents? Doubts seemed rather a strong way to put it, he decided. Reservations sounded better. Yes, he had reservations about her parents. He'd already wondered where they'd gotten the money to live on while following their dream. The news about small investors was disturbing. He needed to get more information. He needed to talk to Lisa.

He got his chance later that morning. Lisa was still taking inventory at the store. There weren't any customers, and it looked as though this would be the perfect opportunity to subtly pump Lisa for information about her parents. But he'd barely said good morning before the door opened and his grandmother joined them.

Lisa greeted Ellie with a smile, but Bryce greeted her with a frown. "You didn't mention you planned on dropping by the store this morning."

"Neither did you," Ellie retorted.

"I came to help Lisa with the inventory."

Lisa raised her eyebrows in surprise. This was news to her.

"I came to do the same thing," Ellie stated. "So you don't need to stay and help out, Bryce."

"There's enough work involved for all of us," he replied with a slight grin, knowing his grandmother was trying to get rid of him again. "I bet with all three of us working we could get the inventory finished today."

The prospect of accomplishing that feat was too tempting for Lisa to resist. She took Ellie aside. "Are you sure you don't mind helping out? I thought you didn't like involving yourself with the routine stuff."

"If Bryce can do it, so can I," Ellie maintained.

"I only had him help me to keep him busy and out of trouble," Lisa explained, not wanting Ellie to feel left out.

"I'm hoping to keep him out of trouble, too. The same goes for you. I'm trying to keep you both out of trouble."

"What do you mean?"

Bryce cut into their discussion. "Are you two going to stand there gossiping in the corner, or are we going to get this inventory done today?"

"We're going to get this inventory done," Lisa said. "Right, Ellie?"

"Right."

Bryce cleverly arranged it so that he was counting the stuffed animals on the top bins, which kept him close to Lisa, who was working nearby. "You know, our trip to Columbia really left me wanting to learn more about gold prospecting," he said with just the right amount of casualness.

"Really? If that's the case, there are some good books on the subject."

"I thought maybe you could tell me more. You've got such a way with words. You make the dull stuff come alive."

The things she went on to tell him were educational, he was sure, but not exactly relevant to her parents' gold operation. "Your parents really seemed to get a kick out of what they're doing."

Lisa nodded.

"Did your father have to do a lot of research before he started?"

"Actually, my father got bitten by the gold bug first, and then went back and read everything he could."

Once Bryce got her talking, it wasn't that hard for him to find out what he wanted to know. According to Lisa, her parents' operation was fairly small but did entail some equipment, such as a dredge and a metal detector. It didn't seem as though Tom Cantrell was interested in expanding the project.

"Daddy's like you," Lisa said. "He's got a way with words. He could probably convince a lot of people to kick in money to enlarge the search, but that isn't what he wants. This is *his* dream, and he can be pretty possessive of it.''

Bryce had heard all he needed to hear. He didn't question Lisa further, at least not about her parents. But Ellie did.

Lisa had just completed the section she was inventorying when Ellie asked her for some clarification on the record sheet. Once Lisa had confirmed that Ellie was indeed doing the recording correctly, Ellie got down to brass tacks.

''Bryce tells me he met your parents.''

''That's right,'' Lisa confirmed.

''What did they think of him?''

''They liked him well enough, even though they didn't quite know what to make of him.''

''You and Bryce have been spending an awful lot of time together lately.''

''I guess we have,'' Lisa acknowledged.

''He'll be going back to Chicago in a week, you know.''

''I know.'' *It's too soon. I don't want him to go yet. But if he has to, I want to spend as much time with him as I can before he leaves.* Finally admitting that was a turning point for Lisa. She was tired of thinking about all the complications. She just wanted to enjoy the here and now.

''I'm worried about you two.''

Lisa smiled reassuringly. ''Don't be. I'm tough. So is Bryce.''

''Bryce is what?'' he asked, having overheard the last part of her comment.

''Tough.''

''Yeah, right. I'm sure I look real tough now, with a pink plush rabbit in each hand.''

Lisa grinned. ''Now that you mention it . . .''

''Don't say it,'' he warned her. ''I'm done counting the stuff in the top cages, or whatever you call those open plastic containers. That's a clever way to display the stuffed animals, by the way. Now what do you want me to do?''

Oh, I don't know. Kiss me. Take me in your arms, maybe. Lisa shook her head at her wayward thoughts. Even though she made some logical and proper answer, it was almost as if Bryce had read her mind. He didn't smile. The movement of his lips was more subtle than that. There was just the slightest tilt at the corner of his mouth that, when added to the gleam in his blue eyes, signified knowledge. He *knew* what she'd been thinking, and this was his way of letting her know that he'd been thinking the same thing himself.

So while Ellie's presence did restrict the amount of physical contact between Bryce and Lisa, it didn't affect the visual contact between them. They shared numerous meaningful glances and sideways looks. Lisa even indulged in a few dreamy stares. Bryce's stares were just plain steamy.

Despite the distractions, they did finish the inventory by that evening, just as Bryce had predicted. He wanted to celebrate by taking Lisa out to dinner, but Ellie insisted that she would treat them both to dinner at a Mexican restaurant in town. Ellie played her role of chaperon as effectively as Lisa's parents had the night before. And so it was that another evening went by without him kissing Lisa. Bryce didn't think he could take another one.

The next morning Bryce was surprised and delighted to get a phone call from Lisa. He realized with a start that it was the first time they'd ever spoken over the phone. Her voice sounded warm and slightly husky. He imagined her lying in bed beside him.

At her end of the phone lines, Lisa was doing some imagining of her own. She was still in bed; it was only eight-thirty in the morning and she didn't have to be at the store until noon. She wondered whether she'd caught Bryce in bed, and then she wondered whether he wore pajamas or went without.

"Are you still there?" he asked as her silence grew longer.

"Umm, yes." She blinked the provocative images away. "Sorry about that. As I was saying, Ellie mentioned last night that she had a hairdresser's appointment this morning. I thought this would be a good time to move the rocking horse over to her house. It's ready, but I need your help transporting it from here to there."

"I'll be there in twenty minutes."

"Wait! I'm not even dressed yet."

"In that case I'll be there in fifteen minutes!" He hung up before she could say anything further.

It was a real scramble for Lisa to get showered and dressed. She could tell by the smile on his face when she opened her front door that he'd been hoping to catch her wearing something slinky. Instead, she looked perfectly respectable in a long denim skirt and a demure, embroidered white blouse. She left her hair down, since she hadn't had time to do more than run a brush through it.

"I understand there's a damsel in distress at this address," Bryce stated. He had one hand propped on the doorframe, the other resting on his hip. He was wearing jeans and a white sweatshirt. His hair was still damp from the shower.

"Whatever gave you that idea?"

"I distinctly recall receiving a call for help that woke me out of a sound sleep."

"I'm sorry. I didn't realize you were still sleeping," she said.

"You should be sorry. I was having one hell of a dream. About you. And it was strictly R-rated."

"Blame it on that spicy Mexican food you ate last night. It can give you some very strange dreams."

"Are you speaking from personal experience here? You ate the same food I did. What did you dream about?"

"Nothing."

"Meaning you're not going to tell me, is that it?"

She smiled and nodded agreeably. "That's it, all right."

"It's probably just as well that I don't know. I'm already having a hard time controlling myself around you. I don't need to add fuel to the fire."

"In that case, maybe we should start moving the rocking horse before Ellie gets back from her appointment."

"Maybe we should. But I need a kiss first."

Even though he'd given her fair warning, she still wasn't prepared for the hunger—not only his, but her own. The moment his lips touched hers, she was alive with needs that demanded to be satisfied. It was only a kiss, or was it a thousand kisses all rolled into one? Where did one caress end and the next begin?

She couldn't think. And she didn't want to. She just wanted this kiss to go on and on.

The need for air finally forced them apart, but it was with the greatest reluctance that Bryce lifted his lips from hers. He didn't release her from his embrace. He simply leaned his forehead against hers and murmured in wonder, "You're a pretty powerful lady, you know that?"

"You're not so bad yourself," she whispered. Was that shaky voice hers?

They stood for a moment or two without saying or doing anything further. It was as if they both needed the time to recover.

Bryce sighed, and she felt it down to her toes.

"If I don't let you go now, we're never going to get this rocking horse moved," he muttered. "Which wouldn't make any difference to me, but I suspect it might upset you, so I'm willing to make the noble sacrifice this one time. I hope you appreciate it."

"I do." She rewarded him with another kiss and then quickly pulled away before he could snare her in his arms again. "And Ellie and her new rocking horse will appreciate it, too."

They had to use Bryce's rental car again to accommodate the large wooden horse. Lisa sat in the passenger seat, watching Bryce drive, an activity she'd never found fascinating before. But today the movement of his hands on the steering wheel had her practically mesmerized. To be honest, it was his hands, not his driving, that were the real focus of her attention.

He had nice hands. Sensitive, capable hands. Capable of driving her crazy, capable of caressing her with gentle passion. She closed her eyes, letting her imagination run free.

A moment later, Bryce stopped the car in Ellie's short driveway. Lisa had a little more trouble bringing her erotic thoughts to a halt.

His request for help brought her out of her reverie. "Can you give me a hand here?"

She smiled. In light of her current daydream, his choice of the word *hand* seemed particularly apropos.

Bryce was tugging on the rocking horse, but it wouldn't budge from the car's back seat. "It seems to have gotten stuck on something."

"Hold on a second. I'll reach in from the other side and see what the problem is." A few seconds later, she was kneeling on the back seat of the car. "Ah, I see it. Just a minute." One of the horse's wooden runners had gotten hung up on his jacket, which had been lying on the back seat. "There you go."

She freed the runner, but the jacket slid to the floor along with a pile of papers. She was about to gather the papers back up when she saw her name in large letters on the file folder. Her hand froze as she reached for one of the sheets. Her name jumped out at her from a dozen places. She closed her eyes and then opened them again. There was no mistake. The papers were from an investigator's report on her.

Seeing it hit her hard. Very hard. She'd been kidding herself, forgetting Bryce's real reason for coming to Jamestown. It had nothing to do with seeing his grandmother or seeing the sights. He'd come to get rid of her.

This should have been old news to her. She'd known he'd had the report—or strongly suspected it, at least—yet still it upset her. She was aware of being vaguely surprised, although she wasn't sure at what.

Her self-mocking sense of humor, which had always protected her in the past, had suddenly disappeared. Finding this damn report hurt. And the pain went deep.

"You okay in there?" Bryce asked teasingly. When he saw her get out of the car, holding the report in her hand, he hurriedly dumped the rocking horse. "We need to talk about this." His voice had the wariness of a man speaking to someone who held a dangerous weapon.

"I knew you had something like this, but..." Lisa shook her head rather dazedly.

"Come on." Bryce tried to take her arm and guide her into Ellie's house. "Let's go inside and talk about this."

Lisa pulled away. "But what about the rocking horse? You can't just leave it out here on the front lawn."

"Forget about the damn horse," Bryce exclaimed. "I'm worried about you!"

"It's a little late for that now," she retorted with more of her usual spirit. "I'm tough, and that horse is our first official acquisition for the toy museum."

"All right, all right. I'll get it. Just promise me you won't do anything rash until we discuss this."

"Depends what you mean by rash," she muttered darkly. At the moment she wanted to break something or, barring that, have a good cry. Which was frightening, since she wasn't the type to shed tears.

"Just wait for me inside," Bryce said.

She nodded. She was in no shape to go anywhere else at the moment, anyway. She needed to recover from the shock. The intensity of her reaction was as much a surprise to her as the discovery of the investigator's report itself. She'd let down her guard—that's what it was. She trusted Bryce, forgetting that she'd built that trust on a rug that could be yanked out from under her at any time.

She shivered. The living room was cold. Or maybe it was just her. She headed for the fireplace, knowing Ellie wouldn't mind if she lit a fire. A minute later the log was burning cheerfully, but Lisa was still cold. She braced one had on the mantelpiece as if she needed to hold on to something solid. The living room, with its Oriental rugs and antique furniture, had always soothed her before. She hoped it would do the same now.

As the initial shock began wearing off, Lisa looked down at the report she'd dropped on the coffee table. She thought it only fitting that she finally read what had been written about her. It wasn't good.

When Bryce came in a few minutes later, she was sitting on a chair, facing the fire. He could see that she was reading the report, but he made no move to stop her. He supposed he owed her that much at least. Hell, he owed her more than that. He owed her a complete explanation. He only hoped he could come up with the right words. He, who was known for always saying the right thing, was worried about being at a loss for words.

After she'd finished reading the report, she stood up and handed it back to him. "This is yours."

Bryce angrily tossed it into the fire.

"Very symbolic," she murmured, "but I'm sure your uncle has other copies." She turned away.

Bryce grabbed her shoulders. "Damn it. Talk to me! Yell, throw things, anything. Just don't shut me out this way."

"I can see why you came rushing out to California." Her voice was coolly mocking. "That detective of yours wrote up one hell of a report."

"Lisa, I didn't hire that detective. My uncle did. The first I knew about any of this was when he handed me the report and told me that someone was out to con my grandmother. I read the report and it did sound . . . incriminating."

"So you hopped on a plane and came out here, ready to expose me as a fraud."

"I came out here to find out what was really going on. But that wasn't as easy as I'd thought. For one thing, you weren't at all what I expected. I've already told you, the more time I spent with you, the more convinced I was—and still am—that you're no more a con artist than I am. You'd never hurt Ellie. I know that. But I have hurt you, and I'm sorry about that. I never meant to."

Her temper flared. "Is that supposed to make me feel better? Because it doesn't. I feel like I've had my life summed up in a sleazy little package presented to you and your family for your reading enjoyment."

"My uncle didn't have you investigated because he was looking for some leisure reading material."

"No, he had me investigated because he's paranoid!"

"He's had reason to be. You may not be a con artist, but there are plenty of people out there who are. People who'll do whatever it takes to get a slice of the pie. It's happened several times to our family already. People have tried to curry favor. They've tried to steal, to deal, to finagle their way into the family's good graces. Some have claimed distant kinship. Others want to marry into the family for the monetary rewards. My younger cousin, Colin, recently broke off his engagement to a woman who, it turned out, was only after his money.''

"Just like that report said I was only after my ex-husband's money?'' Lisa countered. "I can tell you one thing—no monetary reward could be worth having to put up with your family!''

"You haven't met them yet.''

"I don't have to. I'm sure you've painted a very accurate picture of them. It's not a picture I like.''

"Now who's being judgmental?''

"You've got one hell of a nerve talking about judgmental after having me investigated! You read that report and concluded, without having ever met me, that I was a gold digger. What that little report omitted saying is that I supported David throughout our marriage, short-lived though it may have been. I didn't take a penny of his parents' money then. But when my earning abilities couldn't keep up with his spending abilities, David walked out. To this day his parents still think I only married him for his money.''

"Because you accepted the divorce settlement? That was a mere pittance compared to their net worth. You could have justifiably gotten a lot more than you did.''

"How do you know about my divorce settlement?''

He was silent a moment before reluctantly admitting, "I checked the court records.''

"Is there anything you *don't* know about me?'' she demanded caustically.

"Is there anything I *do* know?'' he countered. "As you said yourself, the real facts aren't to be found in that report. I know enough about you to know that.''

"What do you want from me?"

"The truth."

"You wouldn't know the truth if it walked up to you and bit you!"

"I've never lied to you," he pointed out.

"No? What about that song and dance about how you cared for me, how you weren't suspicious of me any longer? And all the while, you were secretly checking up on me."

"I didn't lie to you. I do care about you. Damn it, lady, I'm falling in love with you!"

She opened her eyes wide with astonishment, then narrowed them with suspicion. "Your charm's not going to work on me any longer."

"Then maybe this will."

Before she could make any protest, he had her in his arms. A second later his mouth found hers. He wasn't rough, but he was determined. Since she wouldn't believe his words, he showed her how he felt. The kiss reflected everything—the frustration, the attraction, the need, the love. He wooed her with his lips, seduced her with his tongue.

Lisa tried to hold herself aloof, and if he'd embraced her with teasing charm and meaningless kisses, she might have succeeded. As it was, she couldn't doubt the intensity of his feelings. There was more than just desire in the warm pressure of his mouth. He was kissing her as if she were essential not only to his happiness but to his very life.

The warm and familiar taste of him melted her icy reservations. Her arms slipped around his waist as she moved closer, leaning against him. Lisa forgot their differences as she became immersed in the pleasure.

She kissed him as he was kissing her. She embraced him as he embraced her. Passionately. Freely. Fiercely. She let her hands express her thoughts, running her fingers over his shoulders and down his back with joyful curiosity. He felt so solid—lean yet muscular. She wanted to touch him without the interference of the sweatshirt he was wearing. So she slid her hands down to his waist and up, under the sweatshirt. His skin was warm, his muscles rippling beneath her fingertips as she gloried in her newfound freedom to touch him.

Bryce was already touching her, enchanting her. He, too, had grown impatient with the material separating them, and had unbuttoned her blouse. The flimsy and whimsical peach-colored bra felt smooth and delicate beneath his hands. But no smoother than her bare skin.

Unable to resist, he stroked the underside of her breast with his index finger. Her responsiveness humbled him even as it excited him further. He tried to handle her with gentle restraint, but her husky moans of pleasure almost shattered his control. His caresses became bolder yet equally tender as he continued to pay homage to her beauty, first with his hands and then with his lips.

Lisa tangled her fingers in his hair as she held him to her. The tugging action of his open-mouthed nibbles had her shivering with delight. She felt an aching hunger that was magnified by the way his hips were moving against hers with unmistakable intent. The strength of his arousal increased her own desire until she was practically burning up inside.

Bryce was feeling equally scorched. Only the fact that they were in his grandmother's home and the knowledge that she was expected back at any time kept Bryce from finishing what they'd started. He wanted to make Lisa his; he wanted to take her there and then, on the Oriental rug. Knowing that if he didn't pull away from her now, he might not be able to later, he reluctantly lifted his lips from her sweet skin. His hands trembled as he slid her bra back into place and buttoned her blouse.

He looked up to see Lisa grinning at him. He wondered why until he saw how lopsided her blouse was. He sighed, and stepped away, allowing her to refasten it by herself. He was pleased to see that her hands were no steadier than his.

"We've got to talk," he said somewhat huskily.

She nodded.

"Do you believe me now?"

She hesitated.

"Why is it so hard for you to trust me?" he demanded.

"Maybe because I've got more to lose than you do," she murmured quietly.

"I'm just as vulnerable as you are, Lisa. Help me. Talk to me."

She did. Starting with her marriage to David. "I was his token sign of rebellion," she concluded. "I was a way of getting back at his family. When the rebellion was over, so was the marriage."

Bryce asked the question that had been bothering him for some time. "Is he the reason you're so sensitive about being beholden to anyone?"

Lisa shook her head. "No, that came later. Having read the report, you know about the trouble I had at the pet store I worked at in St. Louis."

"Ellie already explained about that," Bryce told her. "The owners fired you because you turned them in for treating the animals inhumanely."

"Well, being fired that way made it difficult to get another job. When I arrived in San Francisco, I didn't have any references. Finally I got a job in an import store. The guy who managed it said he'd take a chance on me and that I owed him one. His idea of repaying a favor didn't match mine, and history looked like it might repeat itself, with my getting fired again. Luckily for me, the manager met someone else who caught his fancy and soon afterward quit.

That's when I learned that it's best to always carry your own weight and not be dependent on others. Favors can be costly."

"There are no favors between us. What are you afraid of?"

"Losing my heart," she admitted softly.

"The same thing's true for me. And it's a scary proposition, I know. But it doesn't have to be a painful one. Just give me a chance. That's all I'm asking. Don't shut me out. Keep an open mind, about me, about us. We've got something special here. I know it, and I think you do, too. Give it a chance. Give *us* a chance. What do you say?"

"What will your family say?" she countered.

"Let me worry about my family."

"They still think I'm a con artist, don't they?"

Bryce sighed. "They don't know you. I'll straighten my uncle out. Don't worry. But there is something I have to tell you."

"What?"

"Unbeknownst to me, my uncle kept the detective on the job until yesterday. Apparently this detective decided to go check out your parents. Now, don't panic. Nothing happened. Not to your parents, anyway. I called them earlier, and they were fine. But the detective got spooked when someone shot at him. Just as I suspected, it was that paranoid neighbor your parents told us about. He saw someone nosing around, and being the prospector he is, he fired a few warning shots to scare the trespasser away. He scared Jones, all right. The guy went back to my uncle with some exaggerated story of your parents trying to shoot him."

Lisa groaned. "And Romeo and Juliet thought *they* had family problems? Your uncle thinks my parents are murderers and they they think I'm—"

"You're the woman I love. And don't you forget it."

She hadn't forgotten. She hadn't gotten used to it yet, but she hadn't forgotten. As for her feelings for him, she shied away from declaring them yet. She'd already revealed so much of herself to him.

Bryce was disappointed that she didn't reciprocate his words of love, but he wasn't discouraged. She felt the same emotion, he knew. She just needed some time. And this disturbance concerning her parents wasn't helping any.

Wanting to reassure her, he said, "I set my uncle straight about your parents. No one will be bothering them again."

"I'd better call them. They must be wondering what's going on. You didn't tell them all this, did you?"

Bryce shook his head. "I thought it might be a little complicated to explain."

"That's putting it mildly. Well, I'll have to tell them something."

Lisa did call her parents, but she decided against telling them everything. For one thing, she didn't have the emotional energy to go through the whole mess again, and for another, she still didn't want them thinking badly of Bryce. She supposed in a way she was protecting him. She didn't lie; that wasn't her way. Instead, she just sort of glossed over everything and in the end didn't tell them anything.

What could she say? That Bryce's uncle was paranoid and had therefore sent out a detective to check on her and subsequently check on her parents? Or maybe that Bryce's uncle was concerned about Ellie? But what would that have to do with her parents? She felt bad about it, but she had no choice but to let her parents go on thinking that their neighbor, Wild Jeb, had simply scared off an intruder.

"Probably just a poor camper or backpacker," her father said, not sounding very concerned about the incident.

Bryce sympathized with Lisa's plight. He knew she hated not being completely honest with her parents, but he couldn't help appreciating her discretion in this instance. They already had enough trouble with his family; he didn't relish having to defend himself to her parents as well. There wasn't much he could do to make amends, but there was one thing....

"Let me talk to your father before you hang up," Bryce requested.

"Why?" she asked suspiciously.

He caressed her cheek with his hand. "Trust me."

She looked into his eyes, trying to read his intentions. But all she saw was his love for her. It was enough. "Uh, Daddy, Bryce would like to talk to you."

Bryce took the phone and got right to the point. "I've been doing some research on gold prospecting, Tom, and I'd like to invest in your operation. How much would you consider as a reasonable investment? That's all? Are you sure? You wouldn't take more? All right, then. Now Tom, the way I see it, if we invested in one of those high-powered dredges and perhaps a power winch or two, we'd be able to triple your productivity. You've already got all your permits and paperwork in order, right? Which permits? Well, it's my understanding that using a dredge or any mechanical equipment in a river requires a permit from the Department of Fishing and Game. You've got that. Good. How about the Bureau of Land Management? You've filed your claim with them? Great. Then I think we should consider hiring some extra help." Bryce went on to outline a one-, two- and three-year growth plan complete with goals and expected returns.

When Tom asked to speak to Lisa, Bryce handed the phone back to her.

"Honey, your young man sounds all full of enthusiasm, but I just don't think it would work," her father told her. "He's talking as if this were a business, not a dream. And

I'm afraid that if he got involved, all his talk about profit margins would take all the fun out of it. Do you know what I mean?"

"I know, Daddy." She'd been stunned by Bryce's offer to invest, even though she suspected what had instigated it. He felt guilty about the trouble his uncle had caused her parents, and this was his way of making it up to them. But she had been surprised at how enthusiastically he'd jumped into the discussion of prospecting options and how much thought he'd already put into it.

"Do you want to tell him, or should I?" her father asked.

"I'll tell him."

"Tell him we appreciate the offer, and it's nothing personal, but it just wouldn't work out."

"I understand. I'll talk to you later, Daddy. Bye."

Bryce was upset that she'd hung up. "But I wasn't done talking to your father yet. I hadn't told him about options for exploring quartz veins—"

"Bryce, we need to talk."

"Is something wrong?"

"My father thinks it would be best if you didn't invest in his operation. It's very small, and he likes it that way. He doesn't want it to be a huge operation."

"Then why is he getting investors?"

"What makes you think he's got investors? No, don't tell me. Your uncle again, right?"

Bryce nodded reluctantly.

"The only investors my parents have are two or three friends who believe in my parents' dream, and want to help if they can, knowing that it *is* a dream. There are no portfolios, no stockholders meetings, no PR campaigns to drum up support. What your uncle calls investors, my father calls close, lifelong friends."

"And since I'm not a close friend, they don't want me investing?"

"No, that's got nothing to do with it. The thing is, your businesslike approach sort of takes the fun out of it for them."

Bryce looked at her in amazement. "I'm being turned down because I'm too businesslike?"

She nodded. "Now, don't take it personally. My father said he didn't mean it as an insult. You just have different approaches to things. My father's got dreams; you've got goals."

"They're the same thing, aren't they?"

"Not in this case, no. A dream doesn't have to be obtainable for you to have it. Possessing that dream is as important as ever having it come true. That's what a dream means to me, anyway. Now, to you, a goal is something you set your sights on and then follow a certain course of action until you attain it. Dreams are magical; goals are more practical. And there's another thing. You can't buy your way out of sticky situations. At least not with me or with my family. I know your intentions were good, but you were mistaken in wanting to use your money to fix something that had gone wrong. We've got our pride."

"Don't I know it." He shook his head ruefully. "All right, I won't bring up the subject of investing in your parents' operation again, although I still don't understand why they turned me down. Was it pride?"

"They would have turned you down because of pride, had they known about your real reasons. As it was, they turned you down because their dreams and your goals weren't the same."

"So we're back to goals versus dreams again, are we?"

"You haven't really grasped what I've been trying to say, have you?"

Bryce was more interested in grasping her, but he kept his hands to himself for the time being. He knew if he touched her now he might not be able to let her go. "Let me get this straight. A goal is something practical, like wanting you to trust me."

"I suppose that could qualify as a goal."

"And a dream would be something like ... wanting you to spend a couple days at Yosemite with me."

"I guess so."

Bryce thought he'd maneuvered that one rather cleverly. "So what do you say? Would you go to Yosemite with me?" When she hesitated, he added, "We could get two rooms if you'd prefer. I just want to spend some time with you away from all this."

"Is that *all* you want?"

"No." He discarded cleverness for candor. "I want to make love to you. I dream of making love to you. All the time. But I guess it's not a goal. You're not a brass ring at the end of the ride, a trophy I'm trying to win. Hell, now I'm probably the one who's not making sense," he muttered in disgust.

"The answer is yes."

He looked at her in surprise. "What?"

"Yes, I'll go with you to Yosemite."

Nine

Bryce looked at Lisa as if he couldn't believe what he'd heard. "Do you know what you're saying?"

"Yes."

"Why? Why are you agreeing to go with me?"

"Because I've been dreaming about making love with you, too. I guess dreams do come true every once in a while," she said.

"I want more than a dream. I want a relationship. Think you can handle that?"

"Think *you* can handle it?"

"Let's find out..." he murmured, and slid his arms around her. "Mmm, I think I can handle it, all right...." He spoke the words against her mouth as he placed a string of kisses across her lips. Things were just beginning to heat up again when Ellie walked in.

"What's going on here?" she demanded.

"Not much, now that you're back," Bryce said.

Lisa hurriedly released herself from Bryce's embrace. Ellie's worried look made Lisa long to reassure her, but the best she could do under the circumstances was distract her. "Ellie, I've got a surprise for you."

"You surprised me, all right."

"You haven't even seen the surprise yet. Close your eyes."

"So you two can fool around some more? Forget it," Ellie said tartly.

"Don't be such a spoilsport," Bryce retorted.

"Stop teasing her, Bryce. Come on, Ellie. Close your eyes."

When she finally did so, Bryce carried the rocking horse out from behind the desk.

"Okay, now open your eyes. Well? What do you think? Do you recognize it? You saw it at an auction we went to, but another dealer bid on it and ended up buying it. When I told him what a worthy cause the toy museum was, he was willing to come to a reasonable arrangement. So here it is, our first purchased acquisition for the museum. What do you think?" she asked again, since Ellie hadn't answered her the first time.

"It's wonderful."

"I wanted to surprise you."

"You certainly did. You and Bryce *both* surprised me. Now, tell me. What's going on between you two?"

Bryce grimaced. "We're a little old for a parental—or in this case a grandparental—talk, don't you think?" He hadn't been this closely monitored even as a teenager in boarding school, and he was finding it difficult adjusting now. When Lisa poked him in the ribs, he sighed and added, "I know you're only asking because you're concerned about both of us, but there's no need to be. Lisa and I have just had a long talk about the situation, and we've reached an agreement. You were absolutely right to trust Lisa. I trust her, too. And because I trust her, I plan on calling Uncle Harold and telling him to butt out of this matter, once and for all."

"He's not going to take very kindly to that," Ellie said.

"I don't suppose he will, but that doesn't matter. He'll get used to it."

Lisa wondered if Bryce was hoping his uncle would get used to her, too. If so, he was more of a dreamer than she was.

Harold called Bryce before Bryce could call him.

"You were supposed to give me an update on the situation out there, Bryce. What did you find out about the Cantrells' mining operation?"

"It's not a mine. They're prospecting in the river."

"I already know that. Didn't you manage to come up with any new information?"

"As a matter of fact, I have. But I'm not sure you're going to like it."

"I knew it! I was right, wasn't I? That Cantrell woman is syphoning off museum funds and diverting them to her parents, isn't she?"

"No, she isn't. And she wouldn't. And her name is Lisa. I'd appreciate it if you'd use it."

"It sounds to me like you're in danger of losing your objectivity in this case, Bryce. Perhaps it's time for you to come home and for us to put someone else on this job."

"This isn't a case, and it's not a job, Uncle. This is a family matter. And speaking of family matters, Ellie has a right to spend her money however she pleases. I came out here to make sure that it was being spent the way she wanted it to be, and it is."

"You weren't sent out there for that reason, and you know it!" Harold blustered.

"That may not have been why I was sent, but it *is* the reason I came. Give it up, Uncle. Grandfather left his money to Ellie because he loved her."

"Bryce, what's gotten into you? I can't believe you allowed that Cantrell woman to affect you this way. You're obviously not thinking clearly. California is having a bad influence on you. You'd better come back to Chicago immediately and we can talk about this face-to-face. It's not a matter to be discussed over the phone."

"I'm not coming back until my two weeks are up, and then I may not be coming back to stay. It depends on how things work out."

"Are you crazy? You're talking nonsense. I want you back here on the first flight tomorrow morning. If you're not on that flight, there might not be a job for you to come back to!"

"If that's the way you want it, fine. I was seriously considering starting a law practice out here, anyway."

"Do you mean to tell me that you'd give up your heritage, turn your back on your family—not to mention your six-figure salary—to start a one-man practice in some hole in the wall in California?"

"I'm not turning my back on my family. Ellie is family, too. Oh, she may not be blood-related, as you're always pointing out, but she's been my family in all the ways that matter. And you're the one who's trying to make me choose. *You're* turning your back on *me*. Think about it, Uncle, before you do or say anything you might regret." Having given Harold that piece of advice, Bryce hung up the phone.

Lisa could sense the tension in Bryce when he came to pick her up for their trip to Yosemite. She was more than a little nervous herself. This was a big step for her to be taking, and she wasn't taking it lightly. Here she was, trusting her instincts again instead of weighing the pros and cons before making a decision. But then, she'd lived most of her life this way; she supposed it was a little late to start changing now.

At least she wasn't foolishly jumping into something without thinking about the consequences. She knew there were difficulties ahead. But she also knew that what she felt for Bryce was something she'd never felt before. It was new, yet felt old. It was exciting, yet comfortable. In her heart this felt right. And in her head, she was able to argue away the worries.

The farther away from Jamestown they got, the more comfortable Lisa felt with her decision to come with Bryce. She'd waffled for so long over what to wear and what to pack that even now she wasn't sure what she'd put in the suitcase and what she'd left behind. She'd settled on wearing her jeans and a western-style shirt with appliques of stars and crescent moons. She'd tossed her denim jacket over the seat, in case she might need it in the cooler, higher elevations of Yosemite. On her feet she wore red cotton socks and a pair of sturdy, if somewhat battered, walking shoes.

Compared to her, Bryce looked ... quiet. He was wearing jeans and another blue polo shirt, this one with some designer's initials on the pocket. He'd brought his nautical-looking sweater along. The yuppie and the hippie. Lisa sighed.

"Did you say something?" Bryce asked.

"No, I was just thinking. It's a beautiful day, isn't it?"

Bryce nodded.

"Is something wrong?" she asked.

He shook his head.

"You haven't said more than ten words since we left Jamestown. Are you having second thoughts?"

"Not at all. How about you?"

She shook her head. "Not really."

"You could sound a little more convincing."

"So could you."

"I'm sorry. I got a call from my uncle this morning, and it got me thinking."

"About what?" She suspected that Bryce was thinking about them. Despite his earlier assurance, she was afraid that he *was* having second thoughts.

To her surprise he said, "I was thinking about setting up a law practice out here. I realize Jamestown is a small town and may not be a suitable location, but Sonora is the county seat, right?"

Lisa nodded.

"So that would probably be a better bet. It's only twenty minutes away. For that matter, Sacramento isn't even all that far away."

"You're thinking of relocating out here?"

"Yes. What do you think of the idea?"

She didn't know what to think. She hadn't planned that far ahead. "What about your family? And your practice in Chicago? You've built a good reputation there."

"I can build a good reputation here."

"In corporate law?"

"That isn't the only type of law I know how to practice. You don't sound very enthusiastic about the idea of my moving out here."

"It's just that this is a major decision and you shouldn't make it hastily. You're talking about radically changing your life."

"Would it make you feel better if you knew that I'd been feeling restless in Chicago for a while now? And that I don't plan on moving here next week. I'm a careful planner, Lisa. I always have been. But there comes a time when you know something is right and you have to take action. I'm not talking about putting all my belongings in a backpack and exploring the high Sierras. I'm talking about expanding my horizons and my business by making a go of it on my own. It would probably take a few months to complete the move, but I want to know what your feelings are about this."

"I don't know what to say. But I do know that you have to want this change for yourself and not for me. Do you really think you could be happy out here? It's a world away from the hustle of Chicago, from what you're used to. Is this really what you want?"

"It's what I want."

"You sound pretty sure about that."

"I am. What I'm not sure of is you," he said.

"You should be. Sure, that is."

"Is that your way of saying you'd like to have me around?"

"I guess I could get used to it," she teased him.

"Your enthusiasm overwhelms me."

"Oh, so it's enthusiasm you want?" She leaned over and blew in his ear, then nibbled her way around his earlobe. "Is that enough enthusiasm for you?"

"Any more and I might drive right off the road."

"Since we're heading into the mountains, I really wouldn't advise doing that."

"Then you'd better stay on your side of the car."

"Look but don't touch, you mean?"

"Exactly. And remember that when we do get to Yosemite, I'm going to do the same thing to you that you just did to me."

"Good. I'm looking forward to it."

She wasn't looking forward to the mountainous driving, however. She hadn't been kidding when she'd told Bryce once that she was afraid of heights. As long as she was in the car, she felt more secure—there was something between her and the vertical drops. But when they stopped at the first scenic outlook and Lisa got out of the car, that reassuring presence was gone.

Bryce stood on the rocky promontory and gazed out at the scenery. To his left was the solid granite hunk of El Capitan, which still had some snow on its flat top. On his right, Bridalveil Fall was easily visible as it tumbled down the rocky mountainside. The view was even more spectacular than he'd imagined.

"So this is Yosemite," he noted appreciatively.

"It certainly is. Yosemite Valley." *Way* down there, she added to herself.

"I'm impressed," he said.

The main thing that impressed Lisa was the distance between her and the valley down below.

"You can't see much of the view from way over there." He held out his hand for her. "Come closer and take a look."

She shook her head vehemently. "No way."

"Why not?"

"Heights," she said succinctly. "I don't like them."

"You're afraid of heights?"

She nodded. "Don't get me wrong. I enjoy the view. It's beautiful. I'd just rather enjoy it from back here. I don't want to get too near the edge."

"Lisa, you must be at least fifty yards from the edge."

"That's close enough."

He smiled. "I guess it is."

"This isn't funny."

"I didn't say it was."

"Then why are you smiling?"

"Because you looked so cute standing there . . ."

"Shivering in my boots, right?"

"That's not exactly how I would have put it."

"But if the boot fits, wear it, huh?"

"I'm glad to see that the altitude hasn't affected your sense of humor any." He walked back to her. "Tell you what, if you get nervous, just grab on to me."

She did so immediately, and she didn't let him go until they were back in the car.

It took Bryce awhile to get acclimatized to her fear. "Look over there," he'd say, without noticing the expanse of nothingness between here and the view over there.

She'd take a quick peek and then mutter, "I'll look when we get down."

She enjoyed the scenery more once they were in the valley. From here she looked up at the towering domes and snow-covered peaks. She preferred it that way.

Since they weren't able to check into the lodge for a few hours yet, they bought some fixings for an alfresco lunch and then they set out on one of the park's many hiking paths. After walking a while, they found the perfect spot for their picnic. A squirrel skittered away as they sat down on a weathered fallen tree that served as both their chair and table.

"Sorry, fella, but this place was reserved," Bryce said.

"And it's got the best view in the house," Lisa added. From this location they could not only see but also hear the thundering of Yosemite Falls.

"Only the best for you." He stuck a straw in a carton of juice. "An excellent year for apple juice," he noted before handing it to her.

"Maybe you would have preferred beer," she said.

"Don't worry about it. This—" he waved an arm at the view "—is intoxicating enough." Then he focused his attention on her, running his hand along her denim-covered thigh. "Just looking at you is intoxicating."

And just being touched by him was breathtaking, she decided. As she nibbled on the crackers and cheese, her thoughts were consumed with Bryce. He was sitting behind her on the log, constantly reaching over her shoulder for the box of crackers that she held in one hand. Sitting astride the log's smooth, time-worn surface the way they were, she knew they were both playing with fire. She didn't care.

Bryce moved closer until a piece of paper wouldn't have fit between them. She leaned back against him, very much aware of his state of arousal. He rested one hand against her hip in a gesture that was possessive and sexy.

Soon more touching then eating was getting done. Unable to resist a second longer, Lisa turned her head so she could kiss him. He was ready for her. His lips consumed hers hungrily, passionately. When he stroked her lips with his tongue, she moaned softly and parted them. He left no portion of her mouth unexplored; seducing her bottom lip, the curve of her upper lip.

Bryce's hands joined in the tantalizing seduction as he slid them beneath her denim jacket to caress her breasts. Excitement flared deep within her, setting up an aching need that made her shiver. She forgot where they were and thought only of continuing the pleasure. Bryce had also forgotten their surroundings, so completely was he caught up in the heated passion of the moment. Unfortunately, their private domain didn't remain private very long. All too soon they were interrupted by the whistling catcalls of a passing group of teenage hikers.

"So much for relaxing in the great outdoors," Bryce muttered.

When they finally did check into the rustic yet ritzy lodge, Lisa was surprised to find that Bryce had reserved a suite that had two connecting bedrooms.

Once they were alone in the suite, he told her, "I don't want you to feel pressured into anything," and she believed

him. How could she not, when she could see how much he
wanted her? But it was more than just wanting; it was loving. Even the way he looked at her had *Love* written all over
it. "Besides, the suite was the only thing they had available
at such short notice. This place is apparently booked months
in advance."

There it was, his practical streak again. Lisa had to smile.
"Sort of like killing two birds with one stone, you mean?"

"Don't talk about killing birds while you're in a national
park. The wildlife is protected here." He added quietly,
"And so are we. In case you were wondering, I've taken care
of it."

"Thanks."

He smiled. "You're welcome."

"So what do we do now?"

"That's up to you."

"Oh." She looked at him and then nervously looked
away. "Maybe we should get ready for dinner."

"Lisa?" Bryce gently freed the strand of her hair that she
was anxiously twisting into a knot.

"What?"

"Calm down. You're worrying too much."

"I am?"

He nodded.

She gave a rueful laugh. "You're right."

"I'm always right," he murmured with a devilish grin.
"Haven't you learned that yet? No, you don't have to answer that. Go and get ready."

In contrast to their lunch, dinner was very elegant but
equally romantic. They ate in the lodge's dining room. Lisa
was so overwhelmingly aware of Bryce and the looks he was
giving her that she didn't even know what she ordered. She
only knew it was good, but not as good as making love with

him would be. She was nervous and excited, anxious and wild with anticipation.

Could he tell that she was relatively new at this and felt somewhat out of practice? Should she tell him? Would that scare him off? She could just imagine the dinner conversation.

Bryce, I haven't done this much.

What? Had dinner?

No. Gone away with a man.

Brilliant. No, she was nervous enough as it was without bringing it into their dinner conversation. At least she felt confident about the way she looked. She was wearing what the fashion magazines called the Sante Fe look—a denim blouse unbuttoned enough to show the lacy top of the white cotton camisole she wore underneath it, and a matching denim skirt with a hint of slip showing under the bottom hem. Now if only she could feel as confident about everything else.

Seeing the varying emotions chasing across her face, Bryce told himself he was glad he'd given her the option of staying in her own room tonight. Of course, he didn't manage to actually *convince* himself—logically he knew he was doing the right thing by not pressuring her too much, but physically he wanted her with an intensity that was almost painful.

Two weeks. He hadn't even known her two weeks, although it felt like he'd known her forever. And if you put together all the time they had spent together, it would probably equal more hours than a working couple got to see each other in a month or two of dating once or twice a week. He mustn't push her, he reminded himself for the thousandth time. This was too important to mess up.

So Bryce forced himself to be noble. He walked her to her door and then chastely kissed her good night. It had to be a chaste kiss, and a very brief one, because anything else and he would have picked her up and carried her straight to bed.

Lisa was pacing in her room. Why had Bryce practically shoved her out of his bed? No, that wasn't fair. He'd been acting like a gentleman. He'd told her he didn't want to pressure her, that he'd invited her to Yosemite with no strings attached.

Bryce was pacing in his room. Did she realize what a sacrifice he'd made for her? Knowing how strongly she felt about being beholden to someone, he didn't want her to feel she owed him anything. He wanted her to give herself to him freely.

He heard the water running in her room.

She heard him getting ready for bed. He turned the light out. That's your cue, she reminded herself. She hadn't put on a nightgown. Instead, she still wore the old-fashioned camisole top and long ruffled petticoat she'd worn to dinner, but that was *all* she wore.

Slowly she turned the doorknob, relieved to find that the door between their rooms was unlocked. Bryce was indeed already in bed. She paused a moment, standing in the stream of light from her room as she wondered what to do next. Once Lisa's eyes were adjusted to the darkness, she realized that Bryce was very much awake. In fact, he was leaning on one elbow, admiring her.

"I've imagined seeing you this way ever since that night at the inn when we were chaperoned by your parents," he murmured huskily. "You were standing in the doorway, and I wanted you so much that I couldn't even think. We were interrupted that night."

"I remember," she whispered.

"Tonight there won't be any interruptions." Having made that announcement, Bryce shoved the covers aside and got out of bed. He padded barefoot across the floor until he was only a few inches away from her. "No interruptions. Only love."

Lisa was speechless. Not because of his words but because of his appearance. He was wearing a pair of navy briefs that hugged his arousal. He was magnificent. And she was suddenly, inexplicably shy.

"Lisa." He lifted her face to his. "No second thoughts."

"It's not second thoughts. It's..." She reached out and hesitantly touched his bare chest, running her fingers from his collarbone down to his navel. "I think you just took my breath away," she murmured with a sexy laugh.

"You like what you see?"

She nodded.

"I like what I see, too," he said. "I'd like to see more." He slid one finger beneath the camisole's strap and slid it off her shoulders. "How do I get you out of this thing?"

"Like this." She showed him how the front fastenings could be undone.

"Allow me." He gently moved her hands aside and took over the job himself.

Lisa shivered as his knuckles brushed against her breasts. He undid one fastening, then two, kissing her shoulder, the curve of her breasts, as his hands moved lower. The sensation was so exquisite she could only close her eyes and enjoy. He caressed her with his lips, seduced her with his wicked tongue. Feverish with delight, she moved against him, sliding her fingers into his hair and holding him closer. When he took the tip of her breast into his mouth, she gasped his name.

"Mmm?" he murmured against her.

"Don't stop!"

She could actually feel his smile.

He lifted his head for a moment. "Like that, do you?"

"Mmm."

"What about this?" He held her in the palm of his hands, stroking the slope of each breast with his thumb. Then he gently blew on the skin he's just caressed with his mouth.

"That's not bad, either," she noted in a seductive whisper.

"Not bad?" He kissed the puckered peak and then blew again.

She almost melted right there and then. "Wonderful, umm, very, very good!"

He drew away from her. "It will be good between us," he promised her.

"I know."

"Are you still nervous?"

She shook her head. "That was anticipation, Bryce. Not nerves. But when you said good night and just left, I thought you didn't want me anymore."

"I've wanted you from the first moment I saw you." He brought her hand to his body. "Can't you tell that?"

She smiled. "I can now, but I couldn't then."

"*Then* doesn't matter. *Now* is what's important."

"I agree. Now I think it's time you went back to bed."

"What?"

"Trust me." She gave him a heated kiss. "Go on. Get into bed. I've got something to give you."

"Will it take long?"

She shook her head.

He reluctantly backed away, keeping his eyes on her.

The camisole was hanging open. With a flirtatious shrug she let it slip off first one shoulder and then the other. Still without saying anything, she undid the fastening ties at the top of her ruffled half-slip until it, too, fell to the floor. Wearing nothing but a smile and a ribbon in her hair, she came toward him. "I'm giving you myself, Bryce."

"The best present in the world." He pushed the covers aside invitingly, and she slipped into bed next to him.

They lay there, facing each other. Bryce ran his hand from the tip of her bare shoulder, up her neck, to her ear—touching her gently. His thumb caressed her cheek in a way that was both tender and seductive. "I still can't believe you're really here with me," he admitted.

"Believe it."

"Maybe this will convince me," he murmured, lowering his mouth to hers.

He kissed her, his lips moving over hers with eloquent desire. His tongue sought out the sweet nectar of her mouth. He gave more than he took, erotically touching the tip of his tongue to the roof of her mouth.

Lisa shivered with delight as without lifting his lips from hers, Bryce gradually shifted until she was beneath him. Her breasts rubbed against his bare chest, the gentle abrasion a loving caress in itself. Their kiss continued, evolving into a series of delicate nibbles that expanded beyond her mouth to include her neck, her shoulders, her breasts.

Each caress, each kiss, was better than the last. Just when she thought she couldn't stand the pleasure a moment longer, Bryce would move on and find some new source of delight. He seemed fascinated with everything about her, the feel of her, the taste of her.

Lisa was exploring him as well, refamiliarizing herself with those places she'd discovered the last time they'd been this close. She slid her hands over his shoulders, intrigued by the shifting interplay of his muscles. She ran her hands through his hair, loving the feel of it, loving him.

His mouth returned to hers, and this time their kiss was a heated exchange, a wild expression of need. The slick undulation of their tongues, the caressing warmth of his hands was a potent combination. It was fire and thunder.

The only drawback was the room's darkness. Although the door from her room was partially open and some light did shine in, the room was still shadowy. Bryce wanted to see her more clearly, but he didn't want to let her go long enough to turn on the bedside lamp. Even that small period of time was too long to go without her now.

Their embrace became more intimate as his legs became entangled with hers. It was only then that Lisa realized he was as nude as she was. She didn't know where to touch him first. So she touched him all over, her caressing hands clearly arousing him further.

When his groan made her aware of that fact, she paused. Maybe she was giving him more pain than pleasure here.

But Bryce quickly disabused her of that notion. "Don't stop." He brought her hand back to his hip. "I want you to touch me."

So she continued exploring him, sliding her fingers over his velvety strength with tentative wonder.

When the pleasure became too much for him to bear, he rolled away. "Time out," he gasped.

She blinked in confusion until she saw him reaching for a packet on the bedside table. She closed her eyes and smiled, imagining what was yet to come. Then Bryce was with her again, ready for her.

Now it was his turn to explore her, and he did so with a skillful sensuality that left her breathless. His seeking fingers found her hidden heat. Lisa quivered helplessly as fluttering pulses of anticipation surged through her body. He caressed her in a way that was darkly erotic and wildly exciting. The ripples of delight grew, until the sensations were so exquisite and so powerful that she couldn't take it any more. She had to have him, all of him, now. She wanted to tell him, but didn't have the breath to do so. Letting her hands do the talking, she reached for him and guided him to her.

He eased forward, making sure she could receive all of him before completing the union. He lay over her, securely sheathed in her inner warmth. She tightened around him as he began moving. The ensuing friction was incredibly arousing to her. Each slow thrust produced an increasing response until Lisa was gasping, barely able to breathe, let alone think. All she could do was feel.

The tension built and, with it, the need to attain something that was just out of reach. It was there. They both knew it; they could both sense it. Coming closer now, faster, fiercer. He searched. She found. And together they experienced a release that was simultaneous and intense. Like a tidal wave, the ultimate peak of satisfaction suddenly crashed over them, sweeping them up, consuming them and then leaving them sprawled together like a pair of storm-tossed lovers.

Ten

"Am I dreaming, or is this real?" Lisa murmured sleepily, rubbing her foot against his leg.

"Feels real to me." He grabbed hold of her leg and draped it over his. "Very real."

"Mmm." She nuzzled her lips against his throat, just under his chin. "Feels real to me, too." She grinned as she shifted slightly, making her movement a seductive invitation. "Why *did* we wait so long?" she questioned with a mischievous smile.

"Beats me," he muttered huskily, running his fingers over her thigh. "But, honey, I can tell you one thing. The waiting is over, and the pleasure is just beginning."

They made love again. This time they took it slow and easy, with plenty of sensual teasing. They joyfully explored the various ways of pleasing each other, drawing out the ecstasy as long as possible before succumbing to the spiraling tension. The conclusion was just as awesome and even more satisfying than it had been before.

They snuggled together afterward, each quietly dazed by what they'd just shared.

"I had no idea..." she whispered huskily. "I never knew..."

"But you were married."

"That was a long time ago, and it never felt like this."

"Surely since then there's been someone?"

She shook her head.

Bryce felt strangely humbled. "But that was..."

"A long time ago, yes, I know. Believe me, I know."

"Why me? Why now?" He knew it was because she loved him, but he wanted to hear the words.

She looked at him with eyes that reflected her innermost feelings. "You know why," she said softly.

"I do?"

She nodded.

He ran a gentle, encouraging hand down her bare back. "You've never been shy about words before."

"They've never meant so much before."

"Tell me." It was half order, half plea.

"I love you." Saying the words gave Lisa an unexpected feeling of peace, as if the battle she'd been waging with herself had finally come to an end.

For Bryce, hearing the words gave him a sense of completion that he'd never felt before. He hugged her close, unable to express himself in any other way for a moment or two. "I love you, too," he finally murmured against her ear.

When she made no reply, he looked down and realized she'd fallen asleep, her head on his shoulder, her hand over his heart.

He smiled and closed his own eyes. The woman he loved, loved him—and as far as he was concerned, all was right in the world.

Lisa woke at first light. Blinking sleepily, she turned to find that Bryce was already awake and watching her.

"Tell me again," he said.

"Tell you what?"

"That you love me."

"You're going to get tired of hearing me say it," she protested.

"Never."

"Never say never."

"You sound like you've got some doubts left. Shall I take care of them?" His hand hovered over her breast before settling on the creamy slope with warm familiarity.

She caught his hand in hers and pressed it against her heart. "I don't doubt this."

"Then what?"

She couldn't tell him; she wasn't sure she knew herself.

"Maybe if we talked about the future," he suggested, "those doubts would disappear."

Lisa didn't think so. Talking or even thinking about the future only made those doubts stronger.

"Let's not talk," she whispered. "There are so many other things we can do."

"Like what?"

"Like take another walk."

"Or?"

"Eat breakfast."

"Or?"

"Make love."

"Bingo."

*   *   *

Bryce was very much aware that Lisa was avoiding discussing their future. But he didn't know why. He would have thought talking about it would reassure her that they would be together, that this wasn't some sort of fling for him. This was real. He wanted to share his life with her. But how could he tell her that when they couldn't even talk about sharing the next few weeks together?

Maybe she just needed more time. Not that time was a commodity he had much of. But what he had, he would give to her. He had another week of vacation coming. He'd take it now. If he still had a job, that is. If not, he wouldn't have to worry about hurrying back to Chicago. There was no one there waiting for him. No attachments, no pets, not even any plants.

He was only now beginning to realize how sterile his life in Chicago had been, how devoid of emotion. It was as if he'd been living in a black-and-white world and had suddenly discovered color. Having made that discovery, he had no desire to return to his former somber lifestyle. He was meant to be with Lisa. He knew it, but she wasn't sure of it yet. She would be. He'd make certain of that.

Lisa was relieved that Bryce didn't press her on the issue of their future. She'd said she just wanted to make the most of today, and he was doing all he could to make sure her wish was satisfied.

After a very late breakfast, they went out exploring. Lisa chose a path that eventually led them to Mirror Lake. The surrounding mountains were clearly reflected in the still water for a view that seemed too perfect to be real. The calm splendor was an inspiring sight, and Lisa was glad she was sharing it with Bryce.

Standing there, surrounded by all that beauty, gave Lisa a new perspective. Everything else, even the difficulties facing them, seemed small and inconsequential when compared with the majestic scenery. His family, their differing backgrounds, all the complications weren't nearly as formidable or insurmountable as Half Dome. And even that rock formation had been climbed and conquered by those who had the perseverance and determination. Good thing she had plenty of both.

The drive back to Jamestown seemed even more beautiful than the drive to Yosemite had been, perhaps because there was no nervousness between them now, so they were able to sit back and enjoy the ride. Bryce pointed out the hillsides covered with California poppies, Sierra thistles and other wild flowers. The world seemed brighter, more colorful to them both.

Even so, Lisa was still sorry to be leaving the magical heights of Yosemite. Soon they'd be back to the real world and all the complications it entailed. That happened sooner than either she or Bryce had expected.

Bryce had just turned onto Main Street in Jamestown when he did a double take and suddenly said, "You know, if I didn't know better I could have sworn that was my uncle we just passed walking down the street."

"What makes you think it wasn't?"

"It couldn't be. He hates to travel. He hasn't left Chicago in all the time I've known him."

"There's always a first time. You said you'd gotten a phone call from your uncle before we went to Yosemite. Did he say anything then about coming out here?"

Bryce shook his head. His uncle had said plenty, and said it loudly, but no mention had been made of his coming to California.

"Did he sound upset?" Lisa asked.

"You could say that."

"What are you doing?"

"Turning the car around. I want to get another look at that guy."

"We could just park and walk."

"I don't want him to see me until I see him."

Lisa thought that sounded more like a rule of guerrilla warfare than a way to greet a family member, but then his family was very different from hers. If Bryce felt more comfortable driving back and forth along Main Street, who was she to complain?

The second time around, Bryce got a good look at the woman walking next the man in question. "It *is* him!"

Lisa frowned. They'd gone by so quickly she'd barely had time to see the guy. "How can you tell? He had his back to us."

"Because that was my Aunt Patricia walking next to him."

"Oh. So, now what do we do? Stop and talk to them?" It seemed like a logical assumption to her.

"First I'm going to drop you off at your house, then I'm going to go talk to them."

"Why drop me off first? What's wrong? Don't you want them to meet me?"

"Absolutely not!"

Bryce's vehemence made her feel like an intruder. "Fine. Then just drop me at the next corner. I can walk home from there."

"Wait a minute. What are you upset about?" Personally, Bryce thought he was the one who had cause to be uneasy. His uncle was up to something, and Bryce wouldn't feel comfortable until he knew what it was.

"I'm upset because you seem in an awful hurry to get rid of me. Are you ashamed to be seen with me or what?"

"You know that's not true." He stopped the car in front of her house and turned to face her. "I love you."

"You have a funny way of showing it sometimes," she muttered.

He trailed one finger down her cheek. "You liked the way I showed it last night and this morning."

"I'm not talking about that. I'm talking about the way you're blocking a part of your life from me and cutting me out of that life."

With an impatient sign he let his hand fall back to his side. "Lisa, you've said yourself that you don't want anything to do with a family like mine."

"I was angry at the time."

"So now you're saying your feelings about my family have changed?"

"Not really. But they *are* your family, and I'm willing to make an effort to get along with them."

"Very noble of you. But I doubt they'll be willing to make an effort to get along with you," he said bluntly. "At least not right away."

"Oh."

He tugged her into his arms. "I just don't want to see you hurt," he murmured in her ear. "I'm trying to protect you."

"Right," she shot back. "We all know how delicate my feelings are."

He smiled. "I know you like to think you're as tough as nails, but I know that this type of situation must bring back bad memories for you. I don't want you any more spooked about our future together than you already are."

"So I'm the damsel in distress again and your uncle is the wicked witch of the west. Is that right?"

"I believe you're mixing your metaphors there, but you've probably got the basic premise right."

"And you're the knight in shining armor?"

He leaned away to look at her. "Don't you think the role suits me?"

"Not when it's your own family you're going to be jousting." She put some more distance between them so she wouldn't be so easily distracted by his touch. "I think I should come with you."

"No way."

"Don't you think this should be a joint decision?"

"No."

"Maybe I could prevent the situation between you all from escalating into a fight," she pointed out.

"What makes you think we're going to fight?"

"Oh, what, you're going to tell me that properly brought up families don't argue, is that it?"

"No, that's not it. We argue a lot. And we say things in the heat of the moment that we might not mean later."

She eyed him warily. "That could be a dangerous trait. Care to be more specific? What sort of things do you say and not mean?"

"I'm not talking about me. I'm talking about my uncle. He blusters a lot."

"I see. And you'd rather he did his blustering in front of you and not me."

"That's right."

She recognized the stubborn set of his jaw. There was no changing his mind. "Well, it is your family. I guess it is your judgment call."

"So you'll wait here for me?"

"I'll wait."

"Thanks." He gave her a quick kiss, but he was already thinking of the impending confrontation with his uncle.

"Will you be coming back here when you're done?"

"Do you want me to?"

"Yes."

"Then I'll be here."

"Have you lost your mind?" Harold demanded. He was facing Bryce in a suite at the Jamestown Hotel.

Bryce hadn't had much trouble tracking his uncle down. There weren't that many hotels in town.

"I'm not the one who's acting unreasonably here," Bryce returned.

"You mean to tell me that going off the deep end for some woman you've only known a few days is acting reasonable? Pardon me, but I beg to differ. You're acting completely out of character. This isn't like you, Bryce. You've always been dependable, reliable, loyal to the family. What's happened?"

"I've fallen in love."

"With this Cantrell woman?"

"Her name is Lisa." Bryce's voice was terse.

"She's nothing but a common gold digger."

Bryce stiffened. "Be careful of what you say, Uncle."

"I'm not saying anything that you wouldn't tell me, were our positions reversed." Harold tried another tack. "Do you realize you're jeopardizing your entire career?"

"I can practice law anywhere."

"Sure you can. Nickel-and-dime stuff. But not the kind of law you're used to practicing. Not the high-powered and important cases. Sure, you can set up a little cubbyhole and make out wills and do estate planning. Or you could take up ambulance chasing. But you're not going to be able to do what you do best. You've made a name for yourself in Chicago. You're handling cases that involve huge sums of money and players from all over the world. Do you honestly think you could be happy going to the bottom of the pile after having been at the top?"

"It was the top of your pile, not mine. I don't plan on being threatened for the rest of my life, or being bribed into staying in line with the dangling carrot of being a senior partner in the firm."

"Is that what this is all about? Your advancement in the firm? Because if it is, I can assure you that you can have that senior partnership you've been waiting for. All you have to do is come back to Chicago with me and it's yours."

"That's what I mean. 'Do as I say, Bryce, and I'll give you a reward. Disobey me and you'll be punished.' I'm tired of those rules, Uncle. I've got dreams of my own to pursue."

"Dreams?" Harold frowned in confusion. "What are you talking about?"

"Oh, I know the concept sounds foreign to you. It did to me, too. But Lisa opened my eyes to all the possibilities in this world, and there are plenty of them."

"She's filled your head with nonsense—that's what she's done."

Bryce shook his head. "I don't know why I even bother. You're not even going to give her a chance, are you? You haven't heard a thing I've said."

"I've heard everything you've said, but you haven't given me one solid piece of evidence indicating that this woman isn't a gold digger."

"Guilty until proven innocent, is that it?"

"That's it."

"You know, Uncle, I don't think this argument is over Lisa at all. I think it's about Grandfather marrying Ellie. This is just a residual bitterness, isn't it. You still can't even accept the fact that Ellie loved Grandfather. After all this time, you still think she's a gold digger, don't you?"

Harold made no comment.

"You're just blind, that's all. You already know what you think. You don't want to be confused with facts."

"I'm the only one who's dealing with facts. You're talking about emotions and feelings here, nothing concrete. No proof."

"You don't want proof. You want the Stephenson money back under your jurisdiction. I feel sorry for you. You've missed out knowing one hell of a woman by ignoring Ellie all these years."

"I know all I care to know."

"And that's it in a nutshell for you, isn't it? The blinders are on, and that's that. Well, I'm not going to live like that any longer, Uncle. My blinders are off, and I plan on making sure they stay that way."

"I'm not the one wearing blinders. You are. You're so blinded by your attraction to this woman that you can't see how she's using you. My God, she thought she was getting a good deal with Eleanor, but that's nothing compared to what she'd get if she married you. It's the oldest trick in the book, Bryce. I can't believe you've fallen for it."

"What you can't believe is that anyone would want anything to do with this family if we didn't have money."

"That's not true. Edward's wife—"

"Is richer than he is. Yes, I know. You saw his marriage as an addition to the family coffers. I don't happen to view things that way. I'm not looking for someone to please the family. I'm looking for someone who pleases me."

"She's got you right where she wants you, doesn't she? Wrapped around her little finger. She's clever, I'll grant her that. All right, have an affair with her if you must. Take her on little jaunts off to Yosemite. But don't do anything foolish like marrying her."

"How do you know about Yosemite?" Bryce's voice was dangerously low.

"Jones told me."

"You had your private investigator following me?"

Seeing the dark anger in Bryce's face, Harold wisely took a step backward. "I was worried about you."

"The same way you were worried about Ellie? Come on, admit it, Uncle. The only thing you're really worried about is the Stephenson money and the family's supposedly good name." Bryce had to pause and take a deep breath before his anger got completely out of control. Now he knew how Lisa must have felt at having her privacy invaded, and that knowledge only fueled his already smoldering temper. "The truth is that Lisa's too good for this family! But I'm going to marry her, anyway. You'd better get used to the idea, Uncle. And if I find out that you've so much as telephoned Jones again or contacted any other investigator, I'll go to the Bar Association and air a little dirty family linen of your own. Do I make myself clear, Uncle?"

Harold nodded in defeat.

Bryce was very quiet when he returned to Lisa's house. She could practically feel the waves of anger emanating from him.

To his surprise, she didn't ask him questions; she just hugged him, sat him down and made dinner for him. It wasn't anything fancy, just a Mexican omelette and a salad, but he discovered he was starving. They ate in the kitchen.

Lisa was pleased to see the Bryce cleaned his dish. He must like her cooking, which was encouraging. It was strange to think they'd declared their love for each other before they'd even shared a home-cooked meal together. But then she'd never been one for doing things in proper chronological order. Bryce, however, was another matter. He was the methodical type.

"What are you thinking?" he questioned softly.

"This is the first time I've ever cooked for you."

"So it is. The food was great."

She hadn't meant to talk about food. She wanted to talk about them, about their future, about his confrontation with his uncle. But it was so much easier to ask him if he'd like ice cream for dessert.

She was surprised to find her hands were trembling as she tried to maneuver the handle to the old refrigerator into place. She'd done this move a hundred times before and never had any trouble with it. She ended up muttering under her breath and kicking the appliance for resisting her attempts to open it.

"Lisa." Bryce had come up behind her so quietly that she hadn't heard him approach. "You can ask me, you know." He turned her so she was facing him instead of the refrigerator. "I won't bite your head off."

"Ask you what?"

"What you've been wanting to ask me since I got here. How it went with my uncle."

"One look at your face and I could tell how it went with your uncle. Look, we don't have to talk about it now if you'd rather not."

"My uncle is a blind fool. I think this situation with you has stirred up his animosity about my grandfather marrying Ellie."

"Maybe you should call Ellie and warn her that Harold's in town."

While Bryce placed the call, Lisa went to her room and turned down the bed. She didn't know if he was staying the night or not.

In the kitchen, Bryce was speaking into Lisa's vintage 1950s phone and telling Ellie that he was indeed spending the night with Lisa. "I'm going to marry her."

"Have you brought up the subject with Lisa?" Ellie asked.

"Not yet. But I will. Soon."

"What are you going to do about Harold?"

"He's here in Jamestown. That's the main reason I'm calling you. I didn't want you to be surprised."

"But he never travels! What's he doing here?"

Seeing Lisa out of the corner of his eye, he said, "I'll come over and explain the whole thing to you in the morning."

After hanging up the phone, he held out his arms to Lisa. "Come here."

She came to him without hesitation. Where before the pace of their lovemaking had been slow and tender, now it was fast and heated. Bryce impatiently tugged her blouse from her jeans as Lisa eagerly unbuttoned his shirt. They left a trail of clothes from the kitchen to her bedroom. By the time Bryce lowered her onto the bed, she was wearing only a pair of panties and a bra, while Bryce still had his jeans on.

"You're definitely overdressed for this occasion," she murmured.

"You have the sexiest voice. And the sexiest hands!" he added with a gasp as she lowered the zip on his jeans.

"Do you think so?"

"I *know* so."

Bryce hurriedly peeled off both his jeans and his briefs while Lisa lay back on the bed and watched him. She was excited by the masculine lines of his body, the hungry passion in his eyes. Smiling, she held out her arms to him. A second later he was there with her, undoing the front fastening of her bra and cupping her breasts in the warmth of his hands.

"So soft, so sweet. See how perfectly you fit in my hands?"

Lisa looked down and was further aroused by the sight of his hands caressing her body.

"Perfect," he repeated as he placed a string of kisses across the creamy slopes of her breasts. Meanwhile, his hands were busy removing her panties, the final barrier between them. "You're so perfect."

Lisa caught her breath as he began caressing her feminine warmth with his fingertips.

"I love the way you make me feel," she said in a sultry whisper.

"How?" He increased the intimacy of his caresses. "How do I make you feel?"

"Wild. Hot. Excited."

"You make me feel the same way." His touch was now boldly erotic and infinitely arousing.

"Bryce!"

"I know, I know. Let it go, honey."

The pleasure he was giving her darkened her eyes. Her face was flushed, her breathing fast and shallow as, moments later, she was completely consumed by the wild pulses of rapture he'd set off within her.

"The next time, I'll be with you," he promised, turning away to fumble for the foil packet he had in his jeans pocket.

"Allow me," Lisa whispered as she helped him.

By the time she was done, Bryce was taut, throbbing with need.

"Lisa, I can't wait!" he muttered.

"You don't have to." Perched atop his thighs, she braced her hands on his shoulders before sliding down onto him, taking him deep within her. Groaning her name, Bryce pulled her into the surging urgency of his hips. Her body was sultry and slick as she tightened around him in a provocatively sensual embrace. Muttering intimate words of encouragement and desire, Bryce urged her on to a faster tempo. Lisa eagerly complied.

Rise and fall. Withdrawal and possession. A sense of urgency, of imminent fulfillment. Higher and higher plateaus of pleasure until suddenly it was all there, pulsing within her.

Feeling as if she were flying, Lisa gripped his shoulders with trembling fingers, her eyes closed in satisfaction at the powerful waves of ecstasy surging through her. The feel of her convulsive movements drove Bryce to the edge of his control. They peaked together.

Their lovemaking had been intense and infinitely satisfying, but later, long after Bryce had fallen asleep, Lisa continued to lie there, staring at the ceiling. She couldn't seem to stop the thoughts from going around in her mind.

She was concerned—no, make that worried—about history repeating itself. She'd had her fill of not belonging, of being considered unacceptable. She liked her life and herself. That had taken years to accomplish. She wasn't sure she wanted someone else coming in and stirring up all those old feelings of doubt and lack of self-worth. Sure, she'd been able to laugh off Bryce's accusations in the beginning, because she hadn't known him then—hadn't been involved. *She'd* known she was innocent, and that was all that had mattered.

But things were different now. Now she was involved. Now she did care. Now she loved Bryce, and facing his family wasn't something she looked forward to. But she knew it wasn't something that could be avoided for long. Sooner or later the confrontation would come, and she could only hope she'd be ready for it when it did.

Eleven

The next morning Ellie called right after Bryce left.

"He's on his way over to talk to you, Ellie," Lisa told her.

"How are you doing?"

"Fine. If it weren't for this problem with his family, I'd be better than fine. Oh, Ellie." Lisa sighed. "I love him. And he loves me."

"I thought as much."

"I know there are bound to be complications...."

"Lots of them. All caused by Harold. You know, this is what I was afraid of," Ellie said. "This is why I didn't push for you two to get together. Not because I don't think you make a great couple, but because of Bryce's family. You've already been through hell once. I didn't want you to be hurt any further. And I didn't want Bryce to be torn between you and his family the way my husband was torn between me and his family."

"But you and Samuel were happy together," Lisa pointed out.

"Yes, we were," Ellie replied. "Sometimes love can conquer all. I hope that will be the case with you and Bryce, too. But in the meantime, I wish there were something I could do to help."

"Just be glad for us."

"I am."

"Tell Bryce that. I think he could really use some family support about now."

"I'm not really family..." Ellie said hesitantly.

"Ellie, Bryce has told me that he considers you to be his family every bit as much as, if not more than, those stuffed shirts back in Chicago. You *are* family. To both of us."

"I think I'm going to cry."

"Me, too."

The two women sniffed in unison and then started laughing.

"We're a pair, aren't we?" Ellie said.

After she'd hung up, Lisa reflected that as far as Harold was concerned, she and Ellie were a pair of gold diggers. At least you're in good company, she thought to herself. Being compared to Ellie was a huge compliment as far as she was concerned.

Lisa had barely taken three steps away from the phone when it rang once again. This time it was her father calling.

"Hi, honey. Just wanted to know how Bryce took the news about not being an investor. I hope he wasn't too insulted."

"He understood, Daddy."

"Good. I'm glad. Now do you want to tell us what's really going on?"

"What do you mean?"

"I realize your mother and I haven't always been the most practical of parents, but we love you very much. We haven't been so wrapped up in our gold fever that we didn't notice the sparks between you and that young man. We're worried about you."

For once Lisa didn't say there was no need for them to worry. She was a little worried herself.

"Would you like to talk to your mother?" Tom hesitantly asked.

"Yeah," she said shakily.

"There, there, dear," her mother said as soon as she got on the line, her soothing tone the one mothers automatically used whenever their children were upset.

"I've done it now, Mom. I've fallen in love with Bryce. He says he loves me, too."

"But he's rich and you're afraid of what his family might say. Is that it?"

"His family's even worse than David's family."

"Have you met them yet?"

"No."

"Then how do you know they're worse?"

"They think I'm a gold digger."

"Then they're stupid!"

Lisa had to laugh at her mother's blunt assertion.

"Well, they are," Anita Cantrell maintained.

"Even so, Bryce has known them all his life. He's only known me for two weeks."

"And you're worried that he's going to side with his family over you?"

"I don't know. I'm worried about a lot of things, I guess. Worried that he might just be seeing me as a way of rebelling against his family, that I just might be a novelty that will soon wear off."

"Bryce didn't strike me as the sort of person who was very rebellious or much interested in novelties," her mother said. "I think you're still talking about David here. But remember that David was a spoiled eighteen-year-old. Bryce is a grown man with definite views of his own."

"I know. I just hate to be the cause of trouble between him and his family. And I hate feeling that I'm a second-class citizen somehow because I don't measure up to their expectations."

"You've certainly gone beyond our wildest expectations. You know your father and I are very proud of you."

"Thanks, Mom. I needed to hear that."

"And if Bryce's family has any other stupid ideas about you, you just have them get in touch with us and we'll certainly set them straight."

"I'm sure you would. Thanks anyway, but this is something I've got to take care of myself."

After hanging up, Lisa continued to wonder exactly *how* she was going to take care of this problem. She felt this was a test, one she wasn't prepared for and didn't have all the answers to. But one thing was certain—Lisa had no doubt in her mind that Bryce's uncle would come looking for her today. From what she'd heard about the man, from both Bryce and Ellie, it was clear to her that Harold was used to taking matters into his own hands. Oh, yes, he would definitely come looking for her.

But this time, she wasn't going to be caught by surprise. No more unexpected visits by disapproving family members as had been the case with David's father. This time *she* was going to go confront *them*. After all, she was no longer a lovesick eighteen-year-old. *No, now you're a moonstruck twenty-six-year-old. So what?*

"So I've got more confidence now, more experience! I'm not going to wait around. I'm going to take charge of my life! I'm going to find Harold before he finds me," she proclaimed as if the sound of her own voice might increase her fortitude.

Reminding herself that it was better to be the hunter than the hunted, Lisa headed for her closet. What did one wear for such an occasion? she wondered with nervous humor. Maybe she should dress all in black, with a hem down to her ankles. Then again, maybe she should give Harold what he was expecting, something outrageous. After fluctuating between the two schools of thought, she finally settled on something in between, a cotton sundress with a floral print. She tied a pink ribbon in her hair, which kept the more stubborn curls away from her face. With a light application of makeup she was ready to face whatever came her way, including Harold.

Bryce had already told her that his uncle was staying at the Jamestown Hotel. It was a simple matter of walking over there and seeing if he was available. As it turned out, she didn't have to ask for him at the desk. He was already standing there, asking for directions to The Toy Chest.

The man turned and looked at her. Dark business suit, cold eyes, commanding demeanor. Yes, this had to be Harold.

But just in case it wasn't, she pleasantly said, "Harold Stephenson?"

"Yes?"

"I'm Lisa Cantrell."

Harold ignored the hand she held out to him. "Let's go upstairs to my suite. We have some private matters to discuss," he stated. Once they were in the privacy of his sitting room, Harold turned to her and said, "I'm glad you came to see me. It saves me having to find you."

"I'm not that hard to find," Lisa replied. "Most people in town know me."

"I doubt that they know what you're really like," Harold retorted. "But that's neither here nor there. I don't care about the people in this town. I care about my nephew. I want you to stay away from him. You can name your price."

"I'm not for sale, Mr. Stephenson."

Harold shook his head in disbelief. "You may have been able to fool my nephew, but you certainly don't fool me. I'm here to tell you that you're not going to get your hands on *this* family's money."

"I don't want your family's money."

"Certainly you do. You want it for that gold operation of your parents."

"Wrong. My father wouldn't want your money. He's quite happy the way he is, which is more than I can say for you. It must be pretty awful having to be so suspicious, always wondering whether people are after you or your money."

"What if I told you Bryce doesn't have any money of his own?"

"I'd be relieved. He might find it hard getting used to at first, but he's intelligent and he tells me he's a damn good lawyer. I believe him. He won't go hungry, I'm sure."

"So you think you've found a good breadwinner to support you and your freeloading family?"

"What I've found is a man who unfortunately comes from a supercilious and bigoted family."

Harold was outraged. "Bryce loves his family! How long do you think this infatuation will last once he's cut off from everything that's familiar to him? If you cared for Bryce at all, you'd realize that you could only do him harm. Do you have any idea how much he'd be giving up for you? A successful practice in Chicago, an impeccable reputation, friends and colleagues with whom he's spent a great deal of

his adult life. Do you really want him to make all those sacrifices for you?''

"I don't want Bryce to make any sacrifices for me."

"Fine. Then get out of his life. I'll make it worth your
while."

Lisa's temper was coming to a boil. "Well, you see, it's
like this, Harry. I can call you Harry, can't I?" She ignored
his sputtering. "You know, Harry, Bryce might be better off
with people who really care about him, the way Ellie and I
care about him, than with people who only see him as one
of the snobbish Stephensons. He is an individual, you know.
Not just part of a family chain. How well do you really
know your nephew, Harry? When was the last time you
spent any time with him?''

"I see him every day at the office."

Lisa waved his words away. "The office? That's business. I'm talking about personal time."

"We have him to dinner once a month."

"Where you talk about business, I'm sure."

"Listen, young lady, you're not going to change the subject on me. My relationship with my nephew is my own
business."

"You're absolutely right. Just as my relationship with
your nephew is *my* own business."

"I've known Bryce all his life. You've known him a few
paltry days. Did he tell you that I sent him out here with the
express intention of getting rid of you? I thought he'd use
that famous charm of his, and when he told me the other
day that he had the situation here under control, I believed
him. But all the while you were spinning your web around
him, weren't you? Well, he may be infatuated with you now,
but that will soon pass, and when he comes to his senses,
he'll regret ever having met you!''

Harold had scored a direct hit. But before she could assess the damage, they were interrupted by the very man they'd been talking about. Bryce did not look pleased to see her, she noted.

"What are you doing here, Lisa?" he demanded.

"I've been listening to your uncle unsuccessfully try to bribe me."

"*She* came to see *me*," Harold quickly pointed out.

"To try to talk some sense into you. Obviously a mistake," she retorted.

"I'm not as easily deceived as *some* members of the family," Harold returned.

Bryce held up one hand. "That's enough. Come on, Lisa. Let's go. I'll talk to you later," he told Harold.

Once they were downstairs, Bryce said, "We need to talk. I'll walk you home."

They didn't speak further until they were in her living room.

"Why did you go see Harold?" Bryce demanded. "I told you to let me handle it."

"I went to see Harold because I knew that if I didn't find him, he'd find me."

"No, he wouldn't," Bryce retorted. "I had things under control."

"The same way you told your uncle that you had the situation with me under control?"

"Did he tell you that?"

"Did *you* tell *him* that?"

"Not exactly."

"Either you did or you didn't, Bryce."

"I did say that, but I didn't mean it the way it sounds taken out of context."

"So you're denying that you were sent out here by your uncle with express instructions to get rid of me?"

"I came out here, as you know, because I was concerned about Ellie. My uncle's interpretation of my actions is strictly his own. Don't tell me we're back on this issue again. We've been over it time and time again." He tilted her chin up with one finger. "I love you. I want to be with you."

"And if you stay with me, you'll be losing your job and your family." She shook her head and moved away.

"I've already told you that I was feeling dissatisfied with things in Chicago before I came out here."

"But you've never argued with your family before, have you?" she asked him.

"We don't always agree on everything."

"No, I mean you've never been so angry that you've broken off contact."

"No."

"You don't know what it's like. I do. I saw what giving up his family, his heritage, did to David. I don't want to see that happen to you. I couldn't bear to see it happen to you. And it would. One day you'd look at me and realize what you'd given up for me. You'd hold me responsible for your unhappiness."

"No, I wouldn't. I'm not the shallow teenager your ex-husband was, and I don't appreciate being compared to him."

"But don't you see? The situation here is so similar. David's family didn't approve of me; your family doesn't approve of me. I'm worried. Hell, I'm scared. This is all happening too fast. I don't want you doing something you'll regret." She took a deep breath, hoping it would give her the strength to say what had to be said. "I think you should go back to Chicago with Harold when he leaves. And before you think I'm being noble, let me add that I'm not saying I think you should *stay* in Chicago. But I do think you need the time in your natural surroundings to make sure you're doing the right thing."

There was a silence for a moment. Then Bryce said, "I was going to tell you that I have to go back."

"Oh." Lisa felt as if she'd been hit over the head with a sledgehammer. "I see."

"No," he retorted in frustration. "You don't see."

"Then explain it to me."

"I can't. Trust is something either you have, or you don't. It's clear to me that despite everything we've shared, you still don't completely trust me."

"You don't completely trust me, either. Otherwise you wouldn't have been checking up on me to see if I'd gone to see your uncle."

"I wasn't checking up on you," Bryce denied. "I was worried about you."

"Worried about what I'd say to your uncle? Or worried about what he'd say to me?"

"Both."

"Well, you don't have to worry anymore," she said. "The confrontation is over and we all survived."

"But will what's between us survive?" he countered.

"That's what I want you to find out in Chicago."

Bryce was gone by the next morning. Lisa felt devastated. It's your own fault, she reminded herself. You told him to go.

To her relief, Bryce did call her later that night. They carefully avoided any mention of their earlier argument, sticking to safe topics, like the weather and his flight. For the first time he told her why he'd gone back to Chicago, mentioning in passing something about a case that had come to court sooner than expected. Lisa was afraid to ask how long the case would go on. She didn't want to pressure him.

Later, right before he hung up, Lisa thought she heard him say, "I miss you." But before she could reply, she heard the dial tone, which left her thinking she must have been mistaken.

Bryce called again the next night and the next. Each time he was friendly yet preoccupied with the case he was working on. There was no further indication that he missed her. He didn't bring up the subject of moving his law practice to California; he didn't bring up much of anything at all. Yet he kept calling.

Lisa had bypassed concern and gone right to anxious depression. For once she was afraid to confront Bryce. She didn't want to rock the boat; she didn't want him to stop calling. So she kept her fears and her concerns to herself and tried to follow Bryce's lead. When he talked about work, so did she. When he talked about family, so did she. They were talking every night but not communicating much at all.

Lisa found herself starting imaginary conversations with Bryce, conversations where he told her he loved her, something he hadn't said since he'd left. Of course, she hadn't said she loved him since then, either. Where did all your confidence go? She'd asked herself on more than one occasion. Where's your courage?

She didn't know. She only knew that she didn't want to lose Bryce completely, not yet. So she tried to be what he wanted, a friendly, cheerful voice at the other end of the phone. No demands, no pressure, no questions. But the stress was getting to her, and after each call, she ended up crying herself to sleep.

Two and a half weeks after Bryce had left, Ellie took Lisa aside. "Listen, you've been morose for days now. Tell you what—why don't you take tomorrow off and do something that will cheer you up? You usually go to Columbia when you're upset, and you usually ride their stagecoach. Why not do that tomorrow afternoon? It is your day off.''

"I don't know. There are other things I should be doing."

But Ellie was adamant. "Go to Columbia. Ride the stagecoach. It will make you feel better. Trust me."

Lisa frowned suspiciously. "Are you up to something, Ellie?"

"Now, what makes you say that?"

"This sudden urge of yours to pack me off to Columbia."

"I'm not packing you off. It's only a few miles down the road, for heaven's sake, not halfway across the state."

Lisa laughed for the first time in days. "All right, already. I'll go to Columbia."

"Good. And be sure to ride the stagecoach. The fresh air will do you good."

Lisa didn't know about the fresh air, but she did feel better as she walked around her favorite gold town. She also felt some of her old spirit coming back. She remembered how happy she'd been spending the day here with Bryce, and she knew how unhappy she was now.

But no longer. She wouldn't keep living in limbo like this. The love she and Bryce had was worth fighting for. And tonight when he called her, she'd tell him that she loved him, tell him that she wanted to be with him.

Deciding to celebrate the return of her decisiveness, she bought a ticket for the stagecoach. She was helped inside by one of the park assistants who recognized her from prior visits.

"Hey, Lisa." The young man, who was dressed in period garb of jeans, blue shirt, suspenders and hat, also sported a full beard. "Haven't seen you for a while. Glad you decided to ride with us again."

"You've done this before?" one of the other passengers asked.

Lisa nodded.

"My two sons are riding shotgun on the roof. Do you think they'll be safe up there?" another passenger asked.

Again Lisa nodded. "They'll have a great time."

"And I thought the seats on a 727 were cramped," another grumbled.

By the time they set off, seven of them were squeezed into the stagecoach's compartment—three passengers on each bench seat, and Lisa on the collapsible seat in the center. She'd decided to let the rookies have the more comfortable seats. As the coach set off down the street, Lisa couldn't help smiling. She felt like a kid again. She was sure the enthusiasm and delight she saw on the faces of the three kids in the compartment matched the expression on her own face. No, it wasn't riding in comfort, but it was riding in style, and it was riding back into the romantic past.

They'd left town and were on the trail leading through the woods when Lisa heard the familiar password. "Holdup!"

The appearance of the roadside bandit was usually the most popular part of the ride. Today was no exception. The kids were enthralled, and even the adults were impressed.

The rider stayed near the lead horses for a while, checking that the driver and the kids riding shotgun didn't have any valuables. Then he yelled into the coach, "Got any gold or silver in there?"

Everyone said no.

"Got a woman called Lisa Cantrell in there?"

Lisa jumped in surprise. "Yes."

"There's a fella out here says he's been looking for you."

Lisa leaned out the coach's window and saw to her surprise that there were two riders rather than the usual one. Both wore blue bandannas over the lower half of their faces and had their hats pulled down low to cover their features. But there was no disguising Bryce's blue eyes as he stared at her hungrily.

She closed her eyes in disbelief. Great, she thought to herself. You're hallucinating now. Not a good sign, Lisa. Bryce was in Chicago. She'd just spoken to him on the phone yesterday.

Then the desperado with Bryce's hungry eyes spoke. "I'm going to have to ask you to step out of the coach, ma'am."

That voice! It *was* Bryce.

While she sat there, stunned, Bryce leaned over and opened the stage door. He calmed the horse with one hand while with the other he took her hand and, in one fell swoop, tugged her out of the coach and up onto his saddle.

"Am I being abducted, sir?"

"I'm sweeping you off your feet, ma'am."

She nodded approvingly. "And doing a damn good job of it, too."

She could see the smile in his eyes even if his mouth was still covered by the bandanna. "Why, thank you, ma'am."

"Shall we hit the road, cowboy?"

"Definitely."

To the accompaniment of applause and a few cheers from the stagecoach passengers, Bryce rode off with her into the proverbial sunset. Actually, he was headed for some privacy.

Ten minutes later the horse was grazing contentedly in a small meadow while Lisa spread delighted kisses across Bryce's face. The bandanna had long since been tugged down around his neck.

"I missed you, lady," he growled. "Hey—" his voice softened with concern "—you're not going to cry, are you?"

"Me?" She sniffed. "Of course not. It's just that I love you so much."

"I love you, too."

Bryce tipped back his hat and lowered his head, his mouth slanting across her parted lips with hungry desire. He took, Lisa gave, and they both shared. Neither wanted the moment to end, but they had to come up for air eventually.

"I can't believe you're really here," Lisa said in a breathless whisper. "I thought you were still in Chicago."

"I wanted to surprise you."

"You certainly did that. Why didn't you tell me you were coming? And why have you been so distant over the phone?"

"I didn't tell you because I wanted to see you for myself. I could feel that you were slipping away from me, and I didn't want that to happen. So as soon as I finished that court case, I called Ellie and told her I was hopping a plane. I told her about my abduction plans, and she seemed to agree that it was a brilliant idea. As for my being distant, I admit I was angry that you didn't trust me when I left, and then when I got back to Chicago I was so busy wrapping up that case that I guess I got a little preoccupied. But I was actually trying to tie up as many loose ends as possible so that I could come back to California and come back to you."

"I can't believe you arranged all this. I didn't even know you could ride a horse."

"I play polo. I'm rather good at it," he admitted.

"That's not all you're good at."

Bryce grinned. "Impressed you with my skills as a road agent, have I? It's nice to know that if my law practice doesn't take off out here, I can always fall back on abducting beautiful women from stagecoaches."

"Oh, no, you don't. I'm the only woman you can abduct, from stagecoaches or anyplace else, for that matter."

"Care to make that official?"

"What do you mean?"

"I'm asking you to marry me, Lisa."

"Really?"

He nodded. "What do you say?"

Her smile warmed his heart and other places, southward:

"I'd say that you've got yourself a wife, cowboy!"

* * * * *

Silhouette Desire ®

1989
IS THE YEAR
OF THE MAN!

What makes a romance? A special man, of course, and Silhouette Desire celebrates that fact with _twelve_ of them! From Mr. January to Mr. December, every month has a tribute to the Silhouette Desire hero—our **MAN OF THE MONTH!**

Sexy, macho, charming, irritating . . . irresistible! Nothing can stop these men from sweeping you away. Created by some of your favorite authors, each man is custom-made for pleasure—_reading_ pleasure—so don't miss a single one.

Mr. January is Blake Donavan in RELUCTANT FATHER by Diana Palmer
Mr. February is Hank Branson in THE GENTLEMAN INSISTS by Joan Hohl
Mr. March is Carson Tanner in NIGHT OF THE HUNTER by Jennifer Greene
Mr. April is Slater McCall in A DANGEROUS KIND OF MAN by Naomi Horton
Mr. May is Luke Harmon in VENGEANCE IS MINE by Lucy Gordon
Mr. June is Quinn McNamara in IRRESISTIBLE by Annette Broadrick

And that's only the half of it—
so get out there and find your man!

Silhouette Desire's

MAN OF THE MONTH . . .

ATTRACTIVE, SPACE SAVING BOOK RACK

Display your most prized novels on this handsome and sturdy book rack. The hand-rubbed walnut finish will blend into your library decor with quiet elegance, providing a practical organizer for your favorite hard-or soft-covered books.

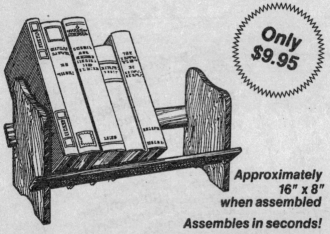

Only $9.95

Approximately 16" x 8" when assembled

Assembles in seconds!

To order, rush your name, address and zip code, along with a check or money order for $10.70* ($9.95 plus 75¢ postage and handling) payable to *Silhouette Books*.

Silhouette Books
Book Rack Offer
901 Fuhrmann Blvd.
P.O. Box 1396
Buffalo, NY 14269-1396

Offer not available in Canada.

BKR-2A

*New York and Iowa residents add appropriate sales tax.

Keepsake

 Harlequin Books

You're never too young to enjoy romance. Harlequin for you . . . and Keepsake, young-adult romances destined to win hearts, for your daughter.

Pick one up today and start your daughter on her journey into the wonderful world of romance.

Two new titles to choose from each month.